Lemon Zest

Lemon Zest

Book I

Perry A. Simpson

© Perry A. Simpson, 2013

Published by The Lemon Zest Project

A CIP catalogue record for this book is available from the British Library.

ISBN 978-0-9926478-0-3

Book layout and cover design by Clare Brayshaw
Cover Image © Rceeh | Dreamstime/com

Prepared and printed by:

York Publishing Services Ltd
64 Hallfield Road
Layerthorpe
York YO31 7ZQ

Tel: 01904 431213

Website: www.yps-publishing.co.uk

I see your smile in every page I write.

Contents

Acknowledgments	ix
Please Read	x
The Weekend Away	1
Albert Smithers	6
Philosophy of Life	11
'Laa Laa' and 'Tinky Winky'	15
The Envelope	19
The Water Leak	23
The Road Traffic Accident	27
The Day That Jack Met Harry	32
The Practical Joker	37
Blueberry Muffins	41
Popcorn	45
The Fog	49
The Lady on the Bridge	53
The Menai Strait	58
Cojones de Toro	63
Lady on the Road	68
Emily Rae	73
The Receptionist	78
Prickly Affair	83
Chance	87
The Perfect Egg	91

The Wall	95
The Bonfire	99
The Secret Recipe	103
Silver Fox	108
Aqua Massage	112
Black Widow	116
The Level Crossing	120
Fire	124
Saucy Jack	128

Acknowledgments

This project has taken several years to reach fruition and I have had help and support from many friends, work colleagues and family along the way. I would like to thank all those that have given some of their time to help turn 'Lemon Zest' from that distant dream into reality.

In particular, I would like to express my sincere thanks to John Worby, Anna Massay and Nick Taylor for helping me iron out those little wrinkles.

Please Read

Dear Reader,

Welcome to Project Lemon Zest.

First, I would like to thank you for your investment in Lemon Zest – By purchasing this book, your financial contribution will help provide a better future for children.

Project "Lemon Zest" started off originally as a book of 30 short stories that I wrote as a personal challenge: 30 stories in 30 days! It was my way of pulling myself out of a period where I was feeling particularly low.

I came up with an idea of writing 30 x 1000 word short stories, designed to provide a short read to accompany a cup of coffee or cup of tea. I was working a twelve-hour day at the time and wrote each and every story in my lunch breaks.

In reality, it did actually take 35 days, due to the fact that I needed to proof read and tweak some of the stories. The challenge became a little more difficult by deciding to write stories of differing genre. The only common factor was that each had a little twist at the end.

The book remained hidden in a folder on my hard drive for quite some time – I had achieved my objective and I was back on track and out of my personal slump.

It wasn't until several years later that I happened to stumble across the folder during a clean up of my hard drive. I read each short story and was quite taken a back – It was of those moments when you cannot believe that you actually did something that impressive. I showed them to a friend who persuaded me to think about publishing them in a book.

Having given this a great deal of thought, I decided to explore the idea and soon became very disillusioned by the difficulties associated with getting a main stream publisher to consider publishing my book. I hadn't intended it to be published and as it was not a very big book in comparison with other short story books or novels that I reviewed, and didn't believe it would be given serious consideration.

I began to explore the world of self-publication and liked the idea of getting more than £1 per copy of the book. However, there appeared to be much bad press associated with the pitfalls of self-publishing. For me, life at the time was already complicated enough without another risky investment – I had made my share of bad financial decisions and I was simply embroiled in debt and did not have the money.

To embark on this self-publishing idea would have meant missing a mortgage payment or two and that wasn't entirely my decision to make. So, I decided to drop the idea all together or at least put it on hold.

Later, I began to reflect on my 50 years of life and asked myself; What am I going to do for the next 50?

I made some very bold decisions and one of these was to work towards my childhood ambition to be a writer. In my line of work as a professional writer and I felt that the transition to fiction would not be that difficult for me.

In addition, I had always said that if ever I found myself in a position of financial stability, then I would like to dedicate some of my time to helping others less fortunate than myself.

From that point, it seemed obvious that I should not just publish "Lemon Zest", but look at this as another one of my projects – A project designed to raise funding for children's charities.

What started out as a little personal challenge 5 years ago is about to take on a whole new purpose in my life – Project "Lemon Zest" was born.

Lemon Zest is a book of 10-minute novelettes designed to provide a 'quick' read during your tea or coffee break. The stories are of mixed genre and each story ends with its own 'unique' twist. The characters are based on 'real' people that I have met in my travels and some of which, my readers may be able to relate to in one or more of the story lines.

I plan to continue writing a series of 10-minute novelette books for the project and some of the characters, together with their story lines will continue in subsequent books. If I was asked to pick a favorite from this book, then it would have to be; 'The Perfect Egg'. Why? It was inspired by a simple idea and I enjoyed crafting the plot, characters and the storyline.

I do hope you enjoy the book and welcome any comments, suggestions and ideas that will allow me to keep this project Lemon Zest 'alive' for many years to come.

Thank you for reading this note and once again welcome to Project "Lemon Zest"

Perry

Blog: http://www. projectlemonzest .blogspot.com
Email: projectlemonzest@gmail.com

The Weekend Away

Tom re-read the letter in utter disbelief, 'What the ...?', he blurted out. Being a solicitor, he knew only too well that it was perfectly genuine and above all – legal. Shaking his head, he tossed the letter onto the leather-top desk, sank deep into his office recliner and slowly slipped into a state of shock. Outside the leaves continued to fall.

Thomas Palmer recalled how he had arranged a weekend away with his long-time friend, Steve Plummer. Although both in their mid-forties, married with grown up children, they were unleashed occasionally, to go away for a skiing, fishing or camping weekend. For Tom, this was a chance to break away from the pressures of his highflying life style; for Steve, an opportunity to play around with loose, carefree women.

The grey clouds grew more menacing, as they began loading up Tom's new metallic grey BMW.

'Looks like we're in for some snow,' said Tom. Steve was about a year older than Tom, but somehow managed to stay younger looking. His almost wrinkle-free face didn't have that permanent weathered expression and only a few grey hairs spoilt his natural wavy, copper-coloured mop.

'It doesn't look promising,' Steve replied.

'I told you we should have set off at lunch time,' Tom snapped.

'I know, but I couldn't get out of the usual Friday afternoon Myers & Stanley sales meeting,' Steve apologised.

'We'll be lucky if we get there at this rate.' Tom paused, looking at the darkening skies. 'We're going to get stranded – I know it,' he added.

'Tom, just shut up you tart and help me with this will you?'

Tom glared at Steve, but knew his slender body mass was no match for the bionic Steve, winner of several small-time bodybuilding competitions. Yet, at school, he was a skinny little runt and all the kids used to bully and tease him, Tom recollected.

He threw a feeble acknowledging glance. Shame that he ended up just a humble paint salesman, Tom thought. Funny how things work out in the end, he smiled to himself.

Soft white fluffy snowflakes began to trickle down from the sky.

◦◦◦

After three hours of driving, those gentle meandering snowflakes grew into a blinding blizzard. Tom eagerly peered through the constant onslaught of large sparkling white dots, desperately trying to find his way. He decided that it was hopeless and pulled into the driveway of a nearby farm.

'Why have we stopped?' asked Steve, suddenly waking from his little nap.

'We are hopelessly lost and I cannot drive any further in these conditions,' Tom snapped, slamming his hands on the steering wheel. His blood-shot eyes watered, as he glared angrily at Steve.

Steve realised that he had not been much help by falling asleep. He should have been assisting Tom by navigating for him.

'What are we going to do now? We cannot stay here – we'll bloody freeze to death,' Tom shouted, digging his nails into the leather cover of the steering wheel.

The snow quickly smothered the surface of the car. Nearby trees drooped hopelessly trying to balance the large white clusters of snow. They both sat in silence for several minutes.

'Well, there is a farm ahead,' Steve announced, startling Tom. 'Maybe, they have a spare room that we could use,' he continued with a glint of hope in his blue eyes.

'Mmm, not sure it's such a good idea ... what if?'

'What are you worrying about? Come on – Leave it to me,' Steve insisted, leaping from the car. Tom found himself staggering through deep snow following Steve's trail as he stomped effortlessly against the blustery blanket of snowflakes. He was heading straight towards the lights of the nearby farm.

'Steve, wait. We can't just stray onto private farmland.'

Steve ignored Tom's whinging and pressed on regardless. He knew that he had to get them out of the cold.

Soon they found themselves approaching an extremely large farmhouse, set in what could only be described, as beautifully landscaped gardens.

'Why is it, that all farmers claim that they have no money?' Steve asked.

'Yes, this must be one of those million-pound estates you read about in "Country Life" magazine,' exclaimed Tom.

Before Tom had a chance to question Steve's next action, the large studded oak door swung open with a slight squeak and an attractive, well-dressed lady appeared.

'Good evening. Really sorry to trouble you like this, but we are hopelessly lost, cold and frightened. Is there any chance of a room for the night?' Steve said, using his usual school boyish expressions.

The lady blushed slightly, paused in thought before answering. 'I realise its terrible weather out there and I have this huge place all to myself, but you see, I am recently widowed,' she explained. 'I'm afraid of what the neighbours might say if I let you stay in my house.'

'We fully understand, my love. Don't worry, we'll be happy to sleep in the barn and I promise we'll be gone before first light. No one will even know. How does that sound?'

Still blushing, the well-groomed lady had no alternative, but, to agree.

Steve took that as a 'yes' and ushered Tom in the direction of a set of adjacent barns. When morning came, the weather had cleared; the welcoming blue sky warmed their cheeks as they set off on their way. They enjoyed a great weekend of skiing.

∽ ∾

Tom suddenly stirred from his coma-like state with a smile, Of course, he thought to himself. He picked up the phone and dialled without pausing.

'Steve, Tom here.'

'Tom, how the devil are you?'

'Fine thanks.'

'How's business?'

'Good.'

'How can I help you, Tom?'

'Steve, I have just received an unexpected letter from a solicitor.'

'Oh,' Steve replied wondering what this might have to do with him.

'Well, it took me a few minutes to figure it out, but I finally determined that it was from the solicitor of that attractive widow we met on the ski weekend nine-months ago.'

'Oh Yes, I remember now, that good-looking lady from the farm.'

'Did you happen to get up in the middle of the night, go up to the house and pay her a visit?' A big smile swept across Tom's face. 'And did you happen to use my name instead of your own?'

Tom tried to imagine the expression on Steve's face, as it reddened with embarrassment. He listened cruelly to his pathetic apologies.

'Steve, it seems that your lady friend died recently,' he paused, 'leaving a considerable sum of money to the charming Thomas Palmer.'

There was a long pause before the line the other end went dead.

Albert Smithers

Albert Smithers lay motionless in the warm hospital bed, surrounded by pale blue walls, the weak scent of daffodils and a choreographed array of bleeps from the modern technology that was keeping him alive. This was the day he had dreaded since the age of five-years old. A warm glow, through the window cast a shadowy spotlight on the mottled carpet, as the tiny rain drops danced on the window ledge outside. In the distance he could hear the mellow shrill of a tiny wren.

Suddenly the door flew open and in marched the very butch-looking Sister Radcliff, closely followed by the very petite Nurse Bartram.

The sister whipped his notes from the holder at the foot of the bed and briskly flicked through the pages. She glanced at him grimly over the top of her glasses. The blank, unconcerned expression on her face said it all.

Albert quietly observed her brash mannerisms. He had noticed that she wasn't wearing a wedding ring and wondered if she had ever had sex with a man. Surely, there isn't a man stupid enough to tackle her, he pondered. If they did, he continued. She would break them during foreplay, he chuckled.

'Father O'Donnell will be in to see you sometime this morning,' she said abruptly.

Albert just nodded. The rain had stopped.

The entourage departed in the same order by which it came in, leaving Albert with only his thoughts once more.

He knew now that he did not have long to live, but the thought of dying still terrified him. He wished that he could turn back the clock, but not because of his fear of dying. Should I mention it to Father O'Donnell? he asked himself. What good would it do now? He sighed.

At that moment there was a gentle tap on the door. Father O'Donnell slipped quietly into the room. He was a very frail old man, with longish grey hair, dark brown eyes and a large cheerful smile. 'My name is Father O'Donnell,' he announced. 'And you might be ...?' he asked.

'Smithers er... Albert Smithers'

'May I call you Bert? It is a little less formal.'

'Of course, be my guest Father.'

'I hear that our dear Lord has called your number?' He paused, 'now, how do you feel about that?'

The question had taken Albert by surprise and he was not quite sure how to answer, 'Well, I do not feel ready.'

'Ah, I see,'

'Do you?'

'Yes.'

'And?'

'How old are you Bert?'

'Eighty-seven, why?'

'When did your fear of death start?'

The question again took Albert by surprise, 'When I was five.'

'Well, let's imagine that you are living your life in reverse. That is, you start out dead and we can get that out of the way.'

'Having not died yet, it is a bit difficult,' exclaimed Albert.

'Bert, please close your eyes and let your conscious mind drift freely.'

Bert closed his eyes and tried to empty his mind.

'You now wake up in a hospital dying of old age, feeling better every day,' the Father continued.

Albert pictured himself slowly getting stronger until the day he was admitted to hospital. He remembered it well.

'Then you get kicked out of hospital for being too healthy.'

Again, Albert tried to imagine being ordered to leave by the butch Sister Radcliffe, being told they needed the bed for someone who is more deserving. He smiled at the thought of her pointing to the door and briskly marching him out of the room, the ward and finally, from the building.

'Enjoy your retirement and collect your pension.'

Albert recollected the many things he had done since he had retired. The trip to the rainforests of Malaysia, the African safaris, the endless tours of the vineyards in France, the operas in Italy, the ride on the Orient Express, the Nile river boat tour, the world cruise, the list seemed endless, he thought. Yes, my pension plan didn't turn out quite so bad after all.

'Then when you retire from work, you get a gold watch on your first day.'

Albert chuckled quietly to himself. I actually did get a gold watch on the first day of my first job.

'You work 40 years until you're too young to work,' said the Father, moving onto the next scenario.

Work – Now there's an interesting one, he thought. I did thirty-years without a single day-off, he continued. Was it worth it? He asked himself. Probably not the most fulfilling part of my life, he concluded.

'You get ready for your final years at school that is. You are drinking alcohol, partying and generally being promiscuous.' the Father continued.

Albert liked the idea of being drunk and getting sober without the hangover. He never had much luck with women. His recollection of this part of his life didn't focus on school, but more on his home life. He still had the scars; the pain never went away. At this point he felt bitter and wanted to move swiftly on.

'Then you go to primary school, you become a kid, you play and you have no responsibilities.'

Oh, Miss Pritchett, he thought. I wonder what ever happened to old rigid knickers. Did she ever marry? Did she ever find out who glued her handbag to the floor, he laughed. She was an old battleaxe, but he decided that in a strange sort of way he liked her.

'Then you become a baby,' said the Father, opening his little black Bible.

Albert could only imagine what it must have been like to be a baby, feeding, sleeping, filling nappies, feeding, sleeping and so on.

'You spend your last 9 months floating peacefully in luxury, in spa-like conditions – central heating, room service on tap and then you finish off as an "orgasm".

This only brought a tiny smile on his face, the only way to go.

The choreographed array of bleeps became a disturbing barrage of alarms. Father O'Donnell whispered, 'I rest my case. May The Lord show mercy on your soul?'

The door exploded as bodies emerged from all directions, but their efforts to revive Albert Smithers were futile. He had given up on living life as he knew it, clinging on to his last thought.

∽✿∾

The Evening Echo read:

"Albert Smithers, better know as 'Smithy', died yesterday at the age of eighty-seven. He spent thirty-years in prison for his alleged involvement in the £30 million bullion heist, back in 1962. A

Lemon Zest – Perry A. Simpson

spokesman at the Royal Gloucester Infirmary said, 'Albert had always protested his innocence right up to the day he died. He was a very quiet man and was very popular with the staff at the infirmary.' The bullion was never recovered.

Philosophy of Life

Professor Gresham stared solemnly into the bottom of his coffee cup and thought how he would miss this small dark musty old office at the university. He gazed through the tired Georgian windows into the mature gardens below, as the autumn winds gathered the fallen leaves. He didn't think that forty years of devotion to philosophy would end like this. He was aware that the university had fallen on hard times, but was it really necessary to weaken the faculty's prospectus? He pondered. His gaze shifted to a brown cardboard box that sat precariously at the end of the table. He reluctantly rose from his mahogany armchair, sliding the box away from the edge of the desk as he did so.

He strolled down the long oak panelled corridor, deep in thought, until he reached the Columbus auditorium. He pushed the double doors open as if making that 'grand' final entrance. Inside, his first-year class sat patiently waiting for their mentor. The Professor placed some objects on the lecture desk; a large empty pickle jar, a box of pebbles and a container of sand. The eyes of his devotees became transfixed on the inanimate objects, wondering what the Professor had in mind for today's lecture, intriguingly entitled the "The Philosophy of Life by Professor Gresham".

A tiny hand rose slowly at the back of the auditorium.

'Yes, Miss Perkins,' the Professor said abruptly.

'Not wishing to be rude sir, but I cannot find today's lecture on the course programme,' she said quietly, peering over her red framed glasses. She pushed her black wavy hair, back behind her ears and nervously shuffled the papers on her desk.

'And what does that tell you?'

Miss Perkins shrugged her shoulders and slid even lower in her seat.

Another hand slowly rose to the ceiling. This time a scruffily dressed male student, named Peter Grace, dressed in jeans, flowery shirt partially obscured by his brown shoulder length hair, grey corduroy jacket and a technicolor woollen scarf.

'Go on Peter, enlighten us,' said the Professor.

'Well, life perhaps never goes as we planned,' he offered, knowingly.

'Yes, looking at your dress code, your mother must be wondering where she went wrong.'

The room erupted into laughter.

'Well, sadly today will be the last lecture that you will receive from me,' the professor announced. He offered no explanation. The students looked at one another. 'It wouldn't be right to leave you lot alone in the sea of philosophy without delivering my philosophy of life lecture,' he exclaimed. He placed the empty pickle jar at the front of the podium. Next, he removed several golf balls from his pocket and placed them inside the jar until the jar could take no more.

'Miss Perkins.'

'Yes sir.'

'Is the jar full?'

'Yes, of course it is,' she replied cordially.

Then, he looked at the students. They nodded in agreement. The professor then picked up a box of pebbles, poured them into the jar and shook the jar lightly. The pebbles worked their way into the open areas between the golf balls.

'Well, Miss Perkins, is the jar full now?'

Now feeling somewhat embarrassed, she half-heartedly agreed by turning her head to one side. The rest of the students, now unsure, followed her lead, producing a weak nod of acknowledgement.

Next, the professor then picked up a box of sand and poured it into the jar. Naturally, the sand filled up the available space in the jar. He turned to the entire class once more, 'Is the jar full?'

The students responded with a unanimous 'yes,' with the exception of one; Peter. Muffled voices could be heard as the students exchanged comments.

The professor waited for the class to settle once more. His eyes casually glanced around the auditorium as he produced two cups of coffee from under the table.

One or two heads began to shake in disbelief, while others adopted a confused look.

The professor poured the entire contents into the jar, effectively filling all the remaining empty spaces between the sand. The professor raised his eyebrows and smiled, 'Is it full now?'

The students erupted into uncontrollable laughter.

'Now,' continued the professor, as the laughter subsided, 'I want you to imagine that this jar represents your life.'

Silence fell upon the class.

'The golf balls are the important things; your family, your children, your faith, your health, your friends and your other passions in life,' he said, rotating the jar a full 360 degrees. 'That is,' he continued. 'Things, that, if everything else was lost and only they remained, your life would still be full.' The students listened in awe.

'The pebbles are the other things that matter; your job, your house and of course, your precious car. The sand represents everything else – The small stuff.'

He had their full attention.

'Now, what would happen if you put the sand into the jar first?" he paused momentarily. 'There will be no room for all of the pebbles or the golf balls,' he continued.

The students nodded slowly.

'The same goes for life. If you spend all of your time and energy on the small stuff, you will never have room for the things that are important to you,' the professor pronounced.

The room was deadly silent.

He raised his tone, 'Pay attention to the things that are critical to your happiness. Play with your children. Take time to have medical checkups. Take your partner out to the opera. Take that hour off work to go to the bank. There will always be time to clean the house and wash that car,' he scowled. 'Take care of the golf balls first, the things that really matter. Get your priorities right. The rest is just sand,' he said resoundingly.

While the other students began to murmur amongst themselves, one of the students raised his hand.

'Yes, Peter.'

'What does the coffee represent?'

The professor simply smiled, 'I'm glad you asked me that Peter.' He acknowledged that despite his somewhat odd appearance, he was by far, the smartest student in the class. 'It just goes to show you that no matter how full your life may seem, there will always be room for a couple of cups of coffee with a friend.'

Peter smiled admiringly.

The professor raised his frail arms to command silence in the room, 'Now, when things in your life seem almost too much to handle; when 24 hours in a day are not enough; when you can never seem to make ends meet.' He paused momentarily to ensure he had their full attention. 'Remember the pickle jar and the coffee'.

'Laa Laa' and 'Tinky Winky'

'Tim, I am sorry, but you'll have to go on your own darling'

'But you know that I hate going to these social things without you.'

'I have the most awful headache. I cannot go like this. You go without me – you'll be fine,' she lied.

Tim picked up his furry purple outfit and made his way from the spacious master bedroom into the adjoining en-suite.

Timothy and Sylvia Myers had been invited to a masked fancy dress party. She had been looking forward to it for weeks, but she would have preferred a more formal dinner dance. She looked at herself in the mirror and sighed, I am in my fifties, my tits are getting closer to my belly and my lovely auburn hair is getting greyer by the day. She sighed at the thought that she had added pounds instead of losing some.

She remembered how she had come up with the idea of their going as two of the telly-tubbies; 'Laa Laa' and 'Tinky Winky'. Quite ingenious, she thought. She had even had in-built voice pieces fitted to cleverly disguise their voices. Yes, quite ingenious, she thought once more. And, we do not even have to remove the entire suit to go to the toilet, she continued – Brilliant!

The grating sound of the bathroom fan reflected Tim's sombre mood, as he stared at himself in the full-length mirror. As the steam cleared, the image that emerged was not a pleasant one. 'Who am I meant to be?' he shouted.

'Tinky Winky,' she replied. Very apt actually, she thought. You only seem to have a little tinky winky in the bedroom these days, she smiled.

Tim had to turn sideways to navigate his body through the adjoining door.

She made a slight adjustment to the triangular aerial on his head, 'Go on, off you go or you'll be late,' Sylvia said trying to hide the laughter behind a simulated smile. Tim reluctantly left. Sylvia took some aspirin and slid into bed alone.

༄

After sleeping soundly for about an hour, Sylvia woke. The pains in her head had gone and she was feeling much better. She looked at the clock. It is still early, she thought. Then a wicked idea popped into her head. Tim has no idea what my costume is, she paused. I could slip quietly into the party and ... she continued to develop the idea further.

༄

She arrived, joining the party unnoticed. She admired the large crystal chandelier that sparkled in the centre of the ceiling of the dimly lit grand hall. Tables and chairs, covered with white tablecloths, clung to the perimeter of the room, small candles providing a quite romantic setting. The music was annoyingly loud. She soon spotted her husband in his purple costume, cavorting around on the dance floor. She watched in horror as he danced with every nice 'woman' he could. I hate going alone to these social things indeed. Well, here's one babe you are going to be unable to resist, she proclaimed, thrusting her chest forward. She admitted that she was indeed jealous.

She danced up to him and immediately started making rather seductive suggestions. Tim responded.

As all men did, she thought, by helping himself to little feel of her pert little butt and a cheeky little kiss. The trap had been set, she smiled cheekily.

Sylvia let him go as far as he wished, naturally, since he was her husband. After more drinks he seemed to finally find the courage to whisper a little improper proposition in her ear. She eagerly agreed. They slipped out, quietly passed the security, into the cold moonlit gardens, along the tall hedgerow, until the found themselves in the car park.

Within minutes they were making passionate love on the back seat. The car rocked to and fro, until finally, the telly-tubbies reached their climax. You are certainly no tinky winky tonight, she gasped. Fond memories of their first encounters in the back of her father's Morris Minor filled her mind. I haven't had an orgasm like that in years.

Sylvia reluctantly slipped away from the party just before the official unmasking at midnight. After all, he had no idea that it was his wife he had just successful seduced, she grimaced. I could have been anyone, she realised, feeling somewhat disappointed now.

⚬⚬⚬

Back at the hotel suite, she put the costume away, showered and got back into bed. 'I wonder what kind of feeble explanation he might offer for tonight's outrageous behaviour,' she grinned. Oh, the same old thing, darling. She could hear those oh so familiar words. You know I never have a good time when you're not with me. I've had the best climax in years, as 'Laa Laa' with 'Tinky Winky', but neither of us knew who the other person was, she frowned.

⚬⚬⚬

Sylvia was sitting up reading a magazine, when Tim came bouncing into the room.

Lemon Zest – Perry A. Simpson

'You must have had a good night,' she said knowingly.

'Yes, it was rather an eventful night as it happens,' he replied, throwing the crumbled purple suit into the bathroom.

'What did you get up to without me?'

'Oh – the same old thing. You know I never have a good time when you're not there,' he replied very convincingly.

She felt hurt, but had to admit that she was impressed. Even his body language was convincing. 'Did you dance much?'

'I didn't dance with anyone,' he scowled.

She couldn't contain herself any longer. She leaped from the bed and reappeared from the bathroom holding the purple suit. 'So how the hell did your costume end up in this state,' she demanded.

'Er, well I have something to tell you my love.' He looked embarrassed.

'Go on.' She couldn't wait for this. He really has no idea, does he?

'When I arrived, I met Peter Brocket, Bill Brown and some of the other guys from the club. So we went into the games room and played poker all evening.'

She always knew when he was lying, but he was so convincing. 'You must have looked rather silly wearing this costume,' she said with a touch of sarcasm.

There was a long pause.

'The party was one of those fully masked affairs and they wouldn't let your father in as Henry VIII, so I loaned him my costume. I knew you weren't coming, so I thought why not. I had a spare set of clothes with me.'

Sylvia's face dropped.

'Apparently, the old bugger had the time of his life.'

The Envelope

'You mean surgery?' Janet said suspiciously.

'Yes, I am afraid so Miss Butcher.'

Margaret Butcher remained quite motionless, panicking at the very thought of an operation. The tiny blue plastic screen, draped on its fragile aluminium frame around her bed, offered no real privacy and she felt embarrassment flushing over her body.

'It is an exploratory operation. It is simply routine surgery under a local anaesthetic. I assure you that your mother has nothing to worry about,' Dr J R Hammond said reassuringly.

'But, she has only cut her tongue,' Janet challenged.

'Can you ask your mother to slip into one of these, please? A nurse will be along in a few moments to prepare your mother for theatre,' he said, ignoring her remark.

Janet Butcher stared at her mother, reached for her hand. 'It'll be alright mum,' she smiled. She then glanced up at Dr Hammond as he drifted through the ward. He is a very handsome man, with his tall thin figure, alluring blue eyes, short cut fairish hair and that sexy rasping voice, she thought. He must be in his mid-thirties. But then, Janet had also noticed, that air of authority, when she was in his presence. He certainly, made the nurses jump when he appeared on the ward. She turned back to look at her poor old mother. She could see the terror in her eyes. She couldn't talk owing to the severe swelling of her tongue and simply squeezed out a fake smile.

∽

Dr Hammond had seen his fair share of anomalies in his professional career, but he really had no idea what had caused Margaret's condition. The antibiotics she had taken last week should have taken care of any likely infection. The scans and X-rays revealed nothing that would normally be a cause for concern. It was a puzzle and he did like the occasional medical teaser.

⁓

Margaret was beginning to feel sorry for herself and she was fighting the tears back. She couldn't talk at all now and this was simply horrible.

'Try to relax mum,' her daughter said.

The curtain opened and, as Dr Hammond had said, a nurse had arrived to get her ready. She was a pretty little redhead, 5ft 4 with hazel-coloured eyes, bright smile and bleached complexion. Within minutes, Margaret was being wheeled to the lift by Harry the porter – a non-descript bald mousy little man with brilliant white teeth and an East London accent.

Well, here we go, thought Margaret. She slowly released the tension in her body and let her mind wander. Above her, the strip light fittings began to flash past, as her limousine headed towards the North Wing.

Damn, I left the washing in the machine, she realised. I doubt if Albert will think to check the machine. He doesn't even know how to switch it on, she sighed. She mustered a smile, I hope he remembers to feed the cat and put her outside for the night. Doubt that too. He hates that cat.

The porter took a sharp left and Margaret noticed the change in the colour of the walls from a wish-washy red, to a garish green. Who the hell chooses the colour schemes? She pondered.

Finally, they had arrived. Her heart jumped a few beats and she began to think about this so-called "exploratory operation" as one of the nurses positioned her underneath a large cluster of spot lights. In the shadow behind the lights, she could see an army of bodies making the last minute preparations, with almost military precision. Tears filled the corners of her eyes now. She was scared. What if they have to cut my tongue off all together? She whimpered. Albert would love that, she grimaced. He is always complaining that I talked too much.

The team around her seem to be ready, nodding gaily to each other. Several pairs of eyes with white-masked faces focused on her now. A hand appeared from the shadows behind the lights and placed a mask over her mouth and nose, 'Just breathe normally Margaret,' one of the nurses suggested.

At first she resisted. The doctor had said it would be a local anaesthetic, she remembered. Each reluctant short intake of air, made her drowsier. Their faces became blurred, voices diminished and speech slurred. She felt cold as the room began to spin slowly around her. Everything went black.

ം൭ൟ

Two hours had passed before Margaret started to emerge from her deep sleep. Her head felt light and her green eyes struggled to focus at first. She had no idea where she was. It took several minutes for her memory to warm up. Had it been a dream? She felt a sharp stinging pain in her tongue. It wasn't a dream. Now she could see faces, blurred at first, the images sharpening, until she could see recognizable facial outlines and then the characteristic features of her husband, Albert and her daughter, Janet.

'Hello mum. How are you feeling?'

She wanted to talk, but knew it would be futile in her condition. The swelling had reduced, but she dare not speak for fear of sounding like a drunken housewife. Albert said nothing. He was still in his blue overalls, cap in his hands, and just stared awkwardly at a spot on the floor.

Dr Hammond joined them.

'May I have a few moments alone with your wife Mr Butcher?'

Janet and Albert swiftly left the room.

'Well Margaret, the operation was successful. The surgeons managed to find the cause of your condition,' he proudly announced. He placed a small specimen jar on the unit next to the bed. Margaret stared in horror and then looked at the Doctor, assuming that it was some sort of joke.

'The only explanation I can offer is that there must have been some eggs on the gum strip of that envelope that you licked a week or so ago,' he conjectured. 'These somehow must have found their way into the cut in your tongue,' he continued. 'The warmth of your saliva must have been sufficient for them to hatch,' he concluded. 'We shall need to keep you here for a couple of days, purely as a precautionary measure of course,' he added.

Margaret was glad that she could not speak. She looked at the tiny cockroaches in the jar and felt physically sick.

The Water Leak

'So there is nothing else you can do?' Mildred asked despairingly. The white handset momentarily slipped from her grip. 'I see,' she replied slowing replacing the telephone receiver. She stared through the hall window, feeling empty, dazed and quite suicidal. The rain fell relentlessly from the raging clouds, tumbling across the darkened skies. Mildred Becker was not looking forward to the storm she knew lay ahead. Despite her age, she was still a stunning looking woman. Her fawn hair didn't show any signs of aging and those wonderful hazel-coloured eyes glistened as much as they always had. She had met her husband, Frank, in her teens and fell in love after that first hurried kiss behind the school bike shed. They had been married more than thirty-years now, but nothing had prepared her for this.

Mildred looked long and hard at the figures on the page. It didn't seem possible. I hope I am going to wake up in the next ten minutes to find it was just a bad dream, she thought. She looked at the various photos dotted haphazardly around the tiny lounge, thinking how her marriage to Frank hadn't always been that smooth. Yet, they had survived where many other marriages had failed.

The handsome young Mr. Baker had said that they had done all they could. It was as much a mystery to them, he had said. She glanced wearily at the green-faced clock on the mantelpiece. Frank would be home soon, she thought, slumping onto the cream leather armchair.

❦

The back door suddenly burst open. Assisted by the howling wind, a rather sodden Frank stumbled into the kitchen. Within seconds, a large puddle quickly circled him as he struggled out of his wet clothing. Stripped down to his white vest and matching 'Y' fronts, his bleached body shivered uncontrollably. His sullen eyes summed up his mood. Frank snatched the towel from the rack and tiptoed into the lounge. The warmth of the room bathed his body, while a fearful-looking Mildred watched him in earnest.

'Is there any mail?' he asked.

It was the question that Mildred had been dreading for the past thirty-minutes or so. She really didn't think she could carry on like this much longer. She passed the opened letter to Frank and looked away, avoiding any form of eye contact. She waited.

'How the bloody ...,' he gasped, glancing at Mildred. Her head was still gazing away into the distance. 'They have got to be joking,' he insisted. 'According to the North bloody Thames Water authority we must be using more bloody water than the entire bloody street.'

Here we go. 'Do they know that water is actually free?' she thought.

Frank paced frantically up and down the narrow space in the room, looking for inspiration, a reason, anything to explain the unusually high water bill that would again burn a hole in his pocket.

'Do you know that water is actually free?' he said.

I blame the bloody Tory government, you know, she sighed. She had heard it all before, but she was too tired to argue anymore.

'I blame the Tory government you know,' he continued. Finally, he threw himself into the vacant armchair, opposite Mildred, 'Where is all the water going?' He sneezed.

Mildred shrugged her shoulders. She had no idea. She did not want to say anything for fear of aggravating the situation once more.

Lemon Zest – Perry A. Simpson

'Give them their due Frank,' she replied. 'The water people have been and conducted all sorts of tests. They checked all the pipe work for leaks. You changed all the washers in the taps, the cisterns and so on,' she continued. 'They've even changed the water meter,' she added.

Frank sneezed, but said nothing.

Their little water leak had become an item on the agenda of the local board of Directors; Frank had seen to that, she thought. Mr Baker made regular visits to check all the meters in the street.

Finally, returning from his thoughts, 'What can we do now?'

'Pay the bloody bill I guess,' she snapped.

'I guess so,' he replied, throwing the water bill on the red-carpeted floor in defeat.

∽♋∾

They ate their hearty evening meal in complete silence, neither had the energy nor inclination to say anymore on the subject. Frank didn't feel so good and went to bed early leaving Mildred in peace with her soaps.

∽♋∾

Mildred was up early as usual and had left for work, leaving Frank in bed. She had to be in early that day to organise the buffet for a school play, "Little Red Riding Hood". Later that day she had an appointment with a solicitor – She wanted a divorce.

Frank had taken a turn for the worse and had decided that it would be better to stay at home. He had the flu.

It was shortly after Mildred had left that Frank woke, convinced he could hear running water. Now I'm bloody dreaming about it, he sighed, turning aggressively on his side. He was starting to slip into unconsciousness, when he was sure he heard the distinctive sound of running water. He listened intently. Nothing – I think I must be going mad, he concluded. Once again, he turned on his side in an attempt to go back to sleep. 'There it is again,' he said, sitting bolt upright. 'It's coming from downstairs,' he gasped. He leapt from the bed, wrapped his dressing gown around himself and went onto the landing. He walked tentatively around the top of the balcony, until he reached the top of the stairs. As he slowly descended, he heard a short gush of water. A burglar, he thought. He grabbed a vase and descended cautiously down the stairs.

It's coming from the downstairs toilet, he concluded. Cheeky sod is taking a pee, he grimaced. Frank tiptoed across the red hall carpet. He raised the vase as he slowly pushed the door ajar.

The door made a piercing squeal as it opened.

'I don't believe it,' he gasped. He stood and watched in utter amazement. Perched on the rim of the toilet, a small grey tabby-coloured kitten stood on its hind legs and operated the toilet lever. When the toilet flushed, the little mischievous pet tried to catch the water with an outstretched paw.

The Road Traffic Accident

'This is your first day with Traffic,' PC Timothy Tanwick said with a touch of sarcasm in his voice. WPC Madeleine Jones smiled, but said nothing. Traffic hadn't been her first choice, but she had to escape from the constant sexual harassment from her former divisional chief. She discreetly glanced across the table at her new partner. She noticed how very clean cut he was, short well groomed dark brown hair, matching eyes, tall with average build, age..?, not sure, she thought. She dropped two sugar cubes into her coffee. A sea of blue plastic chairs and white rectangular tables slowly emerged as the staff canteen emptied. This is not what my father had wanted for me, she thought. "Anything, but the force", he had said to her. Perhaps now she was beginning to understand why. With her well-proportioned body, blonde hair and graceful manner, perhaps she should have considered her previous ambitions of a career in journalism. But after her father's death, all she wanted was to follow in his footsteps to bring villains, like the one that had shot him, to justice. She slowly rotated the tired stainless spoon around the rim of the almost white mug. She blew across the top of the hot coffee and then took a small sip. It was still too hot. This was indeed her first day in traffic and she wasn't looking forward to her first RTA. She didn't have long to wait.

'OK, we're on our way control,' PC Timothy Tanwick confirmed. 'Come on, we haven't got time for that now.' Maddy rose abruptly, knocking the mug onto the floor.

'Leave it, we have our first RTA,' he snapped. 'Doris?' he shouted, pointing to the shattered remains swimming in the milky brown solution. Doris grimaced, grabbing her mop and bucket.

'Great start,' Maddy said under her breadth.

They both leapt into the car, Maddy in the passenger side. Tim called control.

'Yes control, can you please confirm the location of the RTA?'

'Three miles North on the main Bessington road?

'On the bend? '

'ETA Fifteen minutes,'

'Roger'

Maddy knew it well. A cold chill worked its way down her spine. Somehow she knew that it was likely to involve a fatality. She braced herself for whatever may lay ahead.

Tim weaved the car dangerously, in and out of the busy morning traffic, often into the path of oncoming vehicles. Maddy gripped the armrest as they narrowly missed a dirty white transit van. The car swerved, mounted a grass verge, spraying mud in the air. Tim skilfully corrected the car and pressed on, continuing through another two sets of red lights, until they were clear of the town centre. They took the next left at the Shakespeare roundabout into Bessington road and on to the infamous black spot.

As they approached the bend, Maddy's heart began to beat faster. At first, it was difficult to see where the accident had occurred. There was only a single faint skid mark on the slightly moistened grass verge. The fog still resisted the morning sun. Beyond the hedge, the faint image of the remains of a motorbike could just be seen in the distance. A damp chill in the air greeted them as they walked towards the scene. Only a few feet away, a body was lying motionless on the newly ploughed field.

Tim quickly took charge of the situation, 'Maddy you take down the details.'

She nodded. As they clambered over the fence, she recognised the distinctive yellow Yamaha bike. It belonged to Ian Thompson. The registration plate confirmed it. The bike didn't look too badly damaged as she drew closer. The paramedics had arrived and were attending to Ian, but she knew it was already too late.

She meticulously wrote down all his personal details. She didn't need to call control for further information about the driver. Maddy already knew his address details, his next of kin and so on. After all, she had been dating him. Broke up only a couple of months ago, she painfully recalled. Maddy tried hard to remain detached; I have a job to do.

Tim rejoined her, 'You OK?'

Maddy nodded.

'The first RTA is always hard, especially when it involves a fatality,' he said, without even a hint of feeling. 'These youngsters will never learn,' he mocked.

'Can I be the one to notify the next of kin?'

'Are you sure?'

'Yes,' she snapped.

'Probably better coming from a woman,' he replied, somewhat surprised by her request.

'His name is or was Ian Thompson. I know his mother,' she added, fighting back the tears.

Tim's mouth dropped as he suddenly realised that she must have known the deceased personally. He was agitated by his own insensitivity. He was aware of the tragic circumstances that surrounded the death of her father and the real reason for her transfer to traffic.

'I'll take care of the paperwork,' he said with a sincere smile.

'No. I would prefer to do it,' she replied.
He understood.

It was the first anniversary of her transfer to traffic. The events of a year ago were in the past and Ian Thompson was just a faint memory.

Maddy had been called to another RTA on the infamous black spot along Bessington road – three fatalities in the past year. As she drove towards the bend, there was that familiar déjà vu feeling. There was a single, familiar skid mark on the moistened grass verge. The fog had lifted sufficiently for her to make out the remains of a yellow Yamaha motorcycle in the field beyond the hedge. Her heart sank. As she clambered over the fence, it was clear that it was in fact, the same yellow Yamaha bike. Ten metres from the bike, the motorcyclist lay motionless in the newly ploughed field. The paramedic shook his head. He was dead. Even before she saw his face, she knew that it was Jack, Ian Thompson's twin brother. In the driver's mirror, she briefly saw the smiling, happy faces of the former playboys, Jack and Ian. Sadness welled up in her eyes, as her father's words echoed in her ears, "This is a dirty business".

A cold chill paralysed her as she proofread her report. The Pathologist's comments were almost identical to that of a year ago: Cause of death – Thought to have been due to a heavy blow to the head, sustained upon impact with the ground. There would be no major bruises or abrasions to the body, except for a small purple mark on the temple, right-hand side – Possibly made by the retaining strap that had been tucked inside of the helmet.

More disturbingly; the collision occurred exactly one year ago, at approximately the same time, in practically the same location, in similar weather conditions, involved the very same bike and the same family lost a son. Maddy spared a thought for the boys' mother, Wendy, sighed and then signed the report and her resignation letter.

The Day That Jack Met Harry

'What is that on your leg Daddy?' Peter asked innocently. Jack Fischer peered at his son over the top his paperback. Peter smiled and continued industriously adding to his sand castle. The question had been expected. Jack knew it would come one day, but as it did so, it struck a nerve, bringing back a painful and chilling memory. Jack had often thought what might have happened had a passer-by, not come his way that night. The bright golden sun sat high in the sky and a warm gentle breeze trickled in, with the soft ripples of the blue sea. A small tern appeared almost frozen as it hovered majestically above the water.

Jack carefully folded the corner of the current page in his book, climbed out of the sun bed and hopped across the hot roasting sand to join Peter, 'Hey that looks good.'

'Do you like it daddy?'

'Yes, it is very good Peter.'

'What is that on your leg Daddy?' remembering that his dad had not answered his earlier question.

'It's called a scar.'

'What's a scar?'

'It is a mark left after you have had a cut or burn,' Jack answered, looking at the grotesque scar that straddled the lower part of his thigh, just above the knee.

'How did you get it?'

'I had an accident,' he replied smiling at the innocence of his son.

His mind flashed back to 10-years ago. He remembered it as though it was only yesterday. A freak storm had broken off a large branch from the old oak tree at the end of the street where they lived, blocking the access to the small cul-de-sac. He remembered how the wind was ripping at the branches, tossing them into the well-maintained lawns. The abnormally large hailstones stripped the foliage from the trees, leaving the trees looking like skeletons. It was as though hell had escaped and was wreaking havoc in the normally quiet and peaceful little village.

'Will I get one?' Peter asked, with a concerned expression on his little face.

'Only if you are naughty.'

'That's what you always say. Mummy does too,' he exclaimed with a frown on his face.

There was a short interlude, while Peter trotted off to collect some seawater in his little blue bucket. Jack watched as the toddler ran to the edge of the water. He bent down to catch the next wave, very carefully, so as not to scoop up sand as well. Jack laughed as Peter wobbled back, water splashed out from his bucket with each step.

He poured the remaining water into his small moat, 'So, that means that you were naughty doesn't it Daddy?'

How can I argue with that? He deliberated. 'No, not naughty, just stupid,' he replied without giving a thought to how it might influence the next question.

'What does stupid mean?'

'Well, let's say it's when you do something that you know you shouldn't.' Peter seemed to be considering his next question. Jack's memory pricked at him again. He had been foolish that night.

'What happened to your leg?'

'I cut it.'

'What did you cut it with?'

'A chainsaw'

'What's a chainsaw?'

'It's a special saw for cutting wood.'

'Why did you cut your leg with a chain saw?'

'I didn't do it on purpose. It was an accident.' Jack could still feel the pain as it ripped into the flesh, stopping at the bone. He remembered how cold he felt as his life was slowly slipping away, the blood seeping from his badly severed right leg. He had been cutting up the fallen branch in an attempt to clear the blocked road, when the blade jammed, kicking back and slicing into his leg.

'Did you go to hospital?'

'Yes'

'In an ambulance?'

'Yes,' Tom didn't remember the ride to the hospital. He was unconscious. His last vision was a burly man staring down at him at the scene of the accident. He later learnt that a Harry Bannister, a builder from Stockport had taken a wrong turning and was looking for somewhere to turn his van around. He found Jack lying in a pool of blood and quickly tied off the bleeding leg, then raised the alarm. Jack survived, though it was several months before he was fully recovered and able to resume a normal life. Harry's misfortune had saved his life. How do you ever repay someone for saving your life, he thought as he had done so many times before. Peter appeared content and had no more questions. Jack returned to his book.

∽◦∾

The Fischer family had enjoyed a really nice day at the beach, but the weather, as predicted, changed from gorgeous blue August skies to a grey wintry assault, with the winds raging and the rain falling heavily now. As they approached the cul-de-sac near their home, Jack saw before him, a very familiar sight – a huge branch, from the very same oak tree, blocking the road ahead. As he drew closer, he noticed the rear end of a small van, poking out from the beneath its leafy grip. Despite his nightmares of the past, he heroically climbed in through the rear door of the van. The driver, a middle-aged man, had been trapped in his seat by the falling branch. He was bleeding profusely from his right leg. As if guided by some strange paranormal force, Jack tied off the badly crushed leg, using his belt. His swift action was enough to save the man's life, the paramedics had said.

Several months later, Jack received a letter. The address was handwritten and the postcode had been added, presumably by the post office. Intrigued, he opened it:

> Dear Jack,
>
> I am not a man who writes letters, so please forgive my feeble attempt. I am a simple hard-working man, who wants little from life. Several months ago, a brave and fearless man rescued me from the clutches of death. I do not know how I can ever repay you. All I can say is thank you from the bottom of my heart.
>
> Yours truly,
>
> Harry Bannister.

The postmark on the envelope was "Stockport". Jack realised then, that this was not the first time the he had met Harry.

Lemon Zest – Perry A. Simpson

I do not know how I can ever repay you.
'You already have Harry.' Jack smiled.

The Practical Joker

Trickling along slowly in the traffic on London's infamous North Circular Road, Fred gazed around at some of the other motorists and wondered what sort of relationships they had with their partners. At the age of 45 he now had the customary few silvery grey hairs, was a proud owner of a John Smith's beer belly and felt as enthusiastic about life as an inmate on death row. The continual challenges of married life had changed him from a determined athletic hopeful, into a solitary man with 2.4 kids.

He remembered how he and Betty had done many things together sharing almost everything. Now, after seven years of marriage, they seemed to be slowly drifting apart. Betty liked to play bridge, while he preferred the more energetic sports like squash, tennis, and football. She went to yoga, while he went for a jog, she liked vegetarian food; but he liked practically everything that went with a good old pint of John Smiths. Politics, don't even go there, he sighed. In fact they now seemed to have very little in common. She doesn't even laugh at my jokes any more, he thought sadly. The thing that really got under his skin was her relentless moaning – It was non- stop from the moment she stepped in the door, till she went to bed. Nothing that he seemed to do was ever good enough. Everybody else, that is her friends of course, are doing better than we are, he signed. Fred tightened his grip on the steering wheel, time to remind her who Fredrick Franks really is.

Before Fredrick Franks got married he had been a bit of practical joker, but he gave up being "one of the lads" the day he fell for Betty. He had come up with what he thought would be a cunning plan to teach her a little lesson. Perhaps she might appreciate me more after this, he thought to himself. The traffic congestion eased a little. The sun had dropped from sight and nightfall had taken its post. The ground whitened as winter's bitter grip grew ever tighter.

Fred parked the blue Ford Focus on the drive and quickly let himself into the house. He knew that Betty was probably already on her way home. Their son and daughter were both representing the school at football and netball respectively.

∽◦∾

Betty was feeling somewhat dismayed by the sudden downturn in her relationship with Fred. She was well aware that he was not happy – It was obvious. She blamed herself. She had everything that she had dreamt about as a young girl leaving school, but it never seemed to be enough. Her frustration always seems to be aimed at Fred, which she knew to be unfair. He works hard and has always put his family first, she admitted. Today, she thought, it is time that we sat down and talked. She planned to prepare a special supper for two, to go with the bottle of Chardonnay she had hidden in her bag. Her marriage, she thought, may depend on what happens this evening. She edged her little RAV 4 through a gap between a red London bus and a black cab, narrowly missing a cyclist. Only a hundred yards or so and she would be home.

∽◦∾

Fred was in position and the stage was set. To an independent observer, Fred knew that this would all seem rather childish, but had concluded, that desperate times require drastic measures. He had rehearsed this over and over again, with military precision. He heard her car pulling onto the drive followed by the unmistakable double bleep of the car alarm. Her heavy footsteps drew closer. Fred took a deep breadth and waited.

'Hello Fred, I'm home.'

No reply.

Betty walked to the fridge and placed the bottle in the ice box at the top of the unit, 'Hello Fred dear, where are you.' The place was unusually quiet, she thought.

No reply.

Betty was unconcerned at this stage. She removed her full-length Burberry coat, folding it gently and then hung it over one of the kitchen chairs. She placed her matching handbag on the cluttered table top.

First things first, I need a little tinkle, she thought. She strolled towards the downstairs bathroom. Is that water I can hear? The hallway was in complete darkness, but she could see the light bleeding from under the bathroom door. It was deadly silent. All she could hear was her own heartbeat. It rose steadily as she slowly pushed the white panelled door ajar. The bright light beyond lit the hallway. She gasped

Bloodstained water was dribbling over the edge of the bath. She took another step forward. Outstretched hands protruded the rim, both with severe lacerations across the wrists. She placed her hands over her mouth, and took another step. She saw a face beneath the water, bulging eyes, and a contorted face. The taps were still running. 'Oh my god – It is Fred,' she gasped.

Fred suddenly burst out from the water. 'Hello', he shouted.

Betty let out a deafening scream, lost her footing on the wet floor, went crashing through the door, glancing her head on the doorframe, as she fell.

Fred sat up and watched hopelessly as Betty knocked herself cold, 'I don't believe this.' He scrabbled out of the bath, slipping over several times, before reaching Betty. He knelt over her, panic slowly taking control. 'Oh shit, have I killed her?'

Hearing the commotion Mrs Hunter, the next-door neighbour, let herself in through the kitchen door to find Fred hovering over Betty. The blood was seeping from an injury on her head. She felt a sharp pain in her chest, gasped for air and then collapsed onto the kitchen floor – Dead.

The sudden realisation of what had happened now made him feel quite foolish.

'Perhaps my practical joker days are over,' he sighed.

Blueberry Muffins

Hidden away in the darkness of the cupboard, Jackie could hear the footsteps getter louder on the terracotta-tiled floor. Heading directly towards me, she gasped, pressing her hands to her mouth. The dark silhouette cast an eerie shadow over the door. There was a pause. Her heart thumped out an erratic overture. The stony silence was broken briefly by the warning shrill of a frantic blackbird. The kitchen window is open, she thought. Hope was all she had left now. The handle of the door began to turn slowly. She counted, one; two; three. Then, forced the door open with all the strength she could muster.

Jackie breathed a sign of relief as she lay in the bath. It had just been a dream, she thought. She was enjoying a warm soak in the bath and must have drifted off. Jackie thought how much more she was enjoying life since they had moved to France. George had reluctantly accepted an early retirement package from Lloyds. They decided to sell up in the UK and buy an old farmhouse in France. The children had fled the nest and set up home with their own families now. Quite by chance, they came across a charming old farmhouse situated in the very unspoilt Dordogne region. This stunning stone-built house was seductively hidden away in a rural setting amid lush green countryside, winding lanes and sleepy villages.

Jackie slid beneath the bubbles, closed her eyes, very content with their new idyllic life. They had escaped the rat race that overwhelmed so many homeowners in the UK. This is no longer just a dream, she thought.

Outside, the sun had risen high, spreading its warm glow across the rows of smiling sunflowers, standing proud around the boundary of the farm. The crickets sang harmoniously and high in the sky two buzzards were gliding effortlessly. A slight breeze tickled the net curtains in the tiny window. Peace, tranquillity and freedom – très agréable, she sighed. Jackie could understand why so many Brits had been lured to the area with its many charms, surprises and hidden treasures.

George had also adapted well to the change of pace, she thought. George had said the fishing here is very good. They had already eaten fresh fish on several occasions – the rewards of the patient fisherman. George also found the weather very agreeable, which in general, was better than in the UK. Being that much further south seem to make a difference, even in the cold winter months, she thought. Yes, it certainly seems to be the idyllic lifestyle we had yearned for, she concluded with a relaxing sigh.

The water was beginning to feel cold by now. Jackie lifted her prune-like hands out of the water, but resisted the urge to climb from the bathtub. Just five more precious minutes, she sighed. A familiar smell greeted her nose – the smell of freshly baked...

'The blueberry muffins', she shouted.

The relaxing, uninhibited bath came to an abrupt end as she rose sharply from the ornate bath, situated in the centre of the room. She quickly grabbed a white towel from the rail, but it was barely enough to cover the prominent features of her body. More concerned about the muffins, than her appearance, Jackie headed down the creaky wooden stairs and into the kitchen below. The air was filled with the aroma of freshly baked blueberry muffins. Her face was met with a hot blast of air as she opened the oven door. 'Good, they're not burnt,' she uttered. Taking a tea towel from the table, she wrapped it around her hand, removed the tray of unspoilt cuisine from the rail and placed it careful on the side to cool.

A car came sweeping into the gravel drive, spraying small stones as a little blue Renault van swung round to park, facing the exit. The driver gave a small toot of the car horn. Pierre, the baker's son, she thought. In panic, she ran towards the cupboard. It was closer than the stairs. I can hide in here until he had gone. Jackie knew that Pierre would let himself in, place the fresh Baguette on the table and leave. It would only be a couple of minutes at most. She listened intently as the footsteps on the gravel grew louder. There was a gentle tap on the door. The door is open, she thought. It is a nice day. The footsteps drew closer. She waited for the sound of the bread being placed on the table and the footsteps returning to the door.

He's heading directly towards me, she gasped, pressing her hands to her mouth. It was now that she realised that in her panic to flee to the cupboard, the towel had fallen and she was completely naked.

His dark silhouette cast an eerie shadow over the door. There was a pause. Her heart thumped faster. The handle of the door began to turn slowly and the door opened with a ghostly squeak.

'Bonjour Madam, EDF.' In the opening of the door stood a little man dressed in blue overalls. He had a clipboard and a small torch.

Blushing, she replied, 'Bonjour monsieur.'

'Le mètre électrique, Madame?'

She pointed to the meter above her head.

The little Frenchman took out his glasses from the top pocket of his overalls, carefully placing them over his nose.

Lemon Zest – Perry A. Simpson

He fiddled with the torch until a flicker of light shone from the end. He pointed at the dials on the large black meter, progressively writing down the readings, while pointing the torch at the meter.

'J'ai pensé que vous étiez le Boulanger,' she said shakily.

'Merci Madame,' he said, with a blank expression. He politely raised his little cap with the tips of his fingers, 'Au revoir, Madame.' He closed the cupboard door and walked slowly from the house and onto the gravel driveway.

'Bonjour monsieur,' George said as he climbed from his car.

The little Frenchman just greeted George with a cheeky smile, paused to raise his cap and then got into the little blue EDF van.

Realising the coast was clear; Jackie slowly crept out from the safety of the cupboard, just as George entered through the back door. George said nothing, just tried to smile through the confused expression on his face.

'Blueberry Muffin, George?'

Popcorn

Sally Tomkins sat at the end of her sick father's bed reading a story to him. She knew that it was pointless. Her father was slowly dying of congestive heart failure or "CHF" to the medical world.

As she recalled from her conversation with Doctor Patel, "It is a condition in which the heart is unable to adequately pump the blood throughout the body and/or unable to prevent blood from backing up into the lungs." He also said, "It's a process that occurs over a period of time, when an underlying condition damages the heart or makes it work too hard, weakening the organ." His shortness of breath (dyspnea) was characteristic of heart failure and the abnormal fluid retention had resulted in swelling (edema) in his feet and legs. Sadly, as a result, he was now non-responsive to family and friends.

His condition had declined to the point where Doctor Patel had discharged him from the hospital to spend the last hours in the comfort of his own home. That was three weeks ago. Her father had always been a stubborn old sod and it seemed as though he was unwilling or determined to die when he was good and ready. Whatever, it had been a long and agonising time for the whole family and she quietly admitted that she would be glad when it is all over. She continued to read to him, while the rest of the family simply waited for the call.

Closing the book, she glanced out of the window now lost in her thoughts. New buds had formed on the fearsome old oak tree. Patchy shades of yellow and violet appeared under the privet hedge, as new crocuses came into bloom. A bright red-breasted robin foraged amongst the leaves.

What shall we do with Popcorn when he's gone? She pondered

"Popcorn" was a small yappy Jack Russell terrier and more importantly, her father's companion and faithful friend. She glanced over at the dog, as he too lay quite motionless. She was concerned about Popcorn. He hadn't eaten in nearly a week. She had taken him to the vets where they gave him an injection and said that they could do little else. Popcorn just slept in his tiny bed, his sullen eyes opening occasionally and seldom rose from this position.

She paused from her thoughts to watch the school children filing from the bus in their blue uniforms. They're at the mere beginning of their lives, she thought. That was me once, she continued. Her mind drifted back to the days when her father was a strong fine figure of a man with his distinctive black hair and big bushy eyebrows. Back then; he was a proud man, forthright and well respected in the accountancy fraternity. She remembered how he had a real head for numbers. He had been a loving father and devoted to the welfare of his family, especially his two lovely daughters, she smiled. However, her mother had told her, that his only regret was not having a son, but he had never ever mentioned it in front of the girls. She often thought what a wonderful couple they had been. Sadly, Mum had died 7 years ago. The memory sent a cold chill down her spine. That had been the saddest day of her life and she still felt some pain. It was an awful way to depart this world and so unfair, she remembered her father saying repeatedly, the day that she died.

Her mother had developed breast cancer at the age of fifty-five. It had been detected during routine screening, but it was too late to treat and she died six-weeks later.

She remembered how it had destroyed her father. Although he tried to disguise it, he was completely lost without her. She also painfully recalled how there were still some comments of disapproval of her mother's marriage to someone so much older than herself. Yet, she thought, no one would have thought that he would out live her. Another tear trickled effortlessly down her cheek.

Sally glanced once more at little Popcorn. His head was set firmly into his tightly coiled body, eyes still closed.

Only popcorn seemed to raise her father's spirits after the sudden death of mum. He was the latest family dog, rescued from the RSPCA. He had got his name as a puppy, because he used go crazy whenever the popcorn maker came out. He would bark non-stop at the popcorn maker, until the last kernel had exploded into the fluffy soft white nugget. The family would watch and laugh at the new puppy, as he ran round and round barking at the popcorn maker. Her father took him for walks three times a day, everyday without fail, sunshine, rain or snow. They were very close.

She rose from her chair, looked at her father's pale-white frail body. Taking his fragile hand, her mind flashed back to the days when he used to walk her to the school bus stop. Another tiny tear rolled from her eye. Outside the clouds stirred. The trees swayed and the blades of grass rippled as the wind flashed across the overgrown lawn.

All of a sudden, he opened his eyes and shouted, 'Come on Popcorn,' startling Sally. She immediately turned to look at her father. His tired eyes, firmly fixed on Popcorn.

Popcorn raised his head and barked several times.

Turbulent clouds parted momentarily allowing a warm glow of sunshine to smile through the bedroom window.

Sally watched knowingly. Her father's eyes finally closed and she felt his pulse slowly fade, and with it, the life from his body. She didn't know how she felt. Both sadness and relief, she thought. The tears came once more. It took several moments for her to gather herself together. She bent down and kissed her father's forehead.

'Goodbye Dad.'

I must call Heather now, she thought.

As she reached for the mobile phone, she noticed that Popcorn's chest was showing no signs of movement. She smiled, thinking that her father and his faithful old Popcorn had just gone on their last walk together.

She smiled, reached for her mobile phone and dialled Heather's number.

The Fog

The fog outside had not lifted and Jennifer Connell felt a little anxious. She hated to drive in these conditions. Glancing up at the clock on the wall, she realised that she would have to set off soon. Mark usually collected Sam, their son, from swimming on Wednesdays, but Mark was in New York on business.

The room was ablaze with light. Since their divorce Jennifer no longer felt comfortable in the house alone. She was up late last night thinking about what she wanted out of life. I have a lot going for me, but.., she thought. I am at a loss to know where to start. She assembled her things, 'coat, scarf, gloves, car keys, mobile and don't forget some lippy.'

As she looked into the oval mirror above the fireplace she was still trapped in her thoughts. She applied a modest layer to each lip.

Look at all the good things I have, but I am completely lost when it comes to looking to the future, she grimaced. I have no idea what I want anymore, she concluded, as she slammed the door closed.

The fog was extremely dense, so much so, that she nearly lost her high heels in the gravel strip in the centre of the driveway.

This is madness,' she said, but I have no choice, she reasoned. For a split second she had forgotten about the divorce. The dense mist swirled around, smothering everything in its path.

Jennifer grudgingly started the Chevy. It roared into life. The engine purred, as she slowly reversed from the drive. The fog swirled around the beast as it rolled into the street. The trees looked creepy and appeared to move as her car edged slowly forward down the street. The weak light from street lamps could barely be seen. It was very quiet.

No one in their right mind would be out in this, she thought.

Jennifer had insisted on keeping the chunky Chevy – She felt safe and secure, pitched that much higher up than the other motorists. The streets were deserted. She hadn't passed single a car.

The pain, frustration and the intense concentration stirred up her emotions once more, why is it, sometimes I feel strong and positive about the future, while other days I feel that life is pointless? Then, there are days when I feel I'm over him and then, I feel I cannot live without him. She had no idea where she was, only that she must be on the main high street in Cambridge.

I wish I could be strong all the time and not get so hung up with jealousy, anger, rage, sadness, loneliness, bitterness and self-pity, she thought.

She had tried keeping a journal of her life since the break-up, but it had only proved to be counter-productive. She always ended up feeling bitter towards him, I just want to let go of those feelings of us being together and simply remain friends – no more than that.

Jennifer recalled how, a year ago, she had a plan and was focused on what she wanted for Sam and herself. I always seemed to be two steps ahead, she groaned. Now, I simply have no idea what the next step is.

She slowed down, desperately looking for something in the street that she recognised. She knew that she couldn't be far from the Shell garage.

The fog, if anything, appeared to be worsening. 'There should be the garage on the right soon,' she said quietly to herself. The Chevy was almost crawling down the street. She glanced at her watch; 10 minutes had passed.

She shook her head, hatred stirring deep inside. I was angry and I still hate him for what he did to me and how he did it, she snapped. We were married for twelve years and I had no idea that he was bisexual. The very thought brought back the embarrassment of it, if divorce wasn't bad enough. She shook her head in dismay.

Her anger suddenly turned to rage, 'Where's that bloody garage?'

She glanced at her watch again; 15 minutes.

The wiper blades made no difference. The fog was still dense and menacing. It danced eerily around the Chevy as it cut through the thick white haze. Jennifer's face was practically pressed up against the windscreen in an effort to see something that she recognised.

Now, I feel like I will never get rid of all this pain, anger, frustration, she continued. Yes, I must learn to move on, but the loneliness is stealing my sanity and slowly driving me crazy.

Her thoughts were becoming more vocal now, 'Sure, I get out when I can with friends, but it's not easy. Everyone knows the sordid circumstances of my divorce,' she said.

Perhaps I have accepted what has happened with my marriage, but I am not sure how Sam feels. 'Sam won't talk about it,' she grimaced. There have been no reports of behavioural problems from the school, she pondered.

'I hate coming home at night to an empty house. If it wasn't for Sam, I think I would go crazy,' she uttered.

'At last,' she gasped.

The garage suddenly appeared ahead. The fog had lifted. The forecourt was deserted and she could only see a solitary figure behind the protective glass of the kiosk.

Somewhat confused, she pulled Chevy onto the forecourt and climbed out of the car. Instinctively, she glanced at her watch – 20 minutes. She had been driving for 20 minutes. Good, I still have nearly 10 minutes to spare. The school is only another half a mile or so, she thought.

'Can have 20 Dunhill, please.'

'That'll be four-pounds.' The irritating hammering noise of the printer echoed in the empty store.

Something didn't feel right. Jennifer scanned the garage forecourt. She couldn't put her finger on it, but she knew something wasn't quite right.

'When did the garage get refurbished? She asked politely.

'How do ya mean?' replied the teenager in broad a Yorkshire accent.

Jennifer's mouth dropped. Now that the fog had completely cleared, she could see the local green direction sign clearly – it read "Harrogate 5 miles".

She checked her watch again and confirmed that she had indeed only been driving for twenty minutes, but amazingly she was only 5 miles from Harrogate and nearly 300 miles from home.

She was speechless for a second.

'Am I really only 5 miles from Harrogate, North Yorkshire?'

'Yes,' he replied with a confused expression on his face.

'My God, Sam,' she uttered in disbelieve. Leaving her change, she ran back to the car and immediately reached for her mobile. Panic slowly took control despite her efforts to remain calm. She furious punched numbers, each bleep acknowledging her selection. While waiting to be connected, she glanced at the sign again.

The Lady on the Bridge

There was barely more than a week and Caroline Harper was beginning to have second thoughts about marriage. Just over six months ago, she had been swept off her feet when Matthew Collins proposed to her. She remembered it well, a wonderful candle-lit dinner at the "Casa Romana" Italian restaurant, set in a rustic setting, which felt just like a traditional Italian villa.

Together, they savoured Italian specialties: Tuscan seafood soup, beef Saltimbocca and home-made prawn ravioli. They finished in style with an amaretto mousse and a glass of grappa.

The ice-cold wind snapped her back from her dreams. The snow was falling heavily now. Large flakes swirled in the blustery winds. An inch of snow had quickly covered the ground with a velvet coat of white. The nearby trees sagged under the weight of their white snowy jackets. The life beneath the surface of the river had been sealed under a thin layer of ice and was now covered with the gentle dusting of snow. As she made her way to the stone bridge, she remembered how, just a year ago, she'd lost the man she had been in love after her stepmother had died. They had grown up together, but only became more than 'just friends' when her mother was taken from her by a rare illness. Perhaps that was the problem, she thought. We were always more like brother and sister. Maybe that is why he didn't show that day, she thought.

As she glanced up towards the bridge, Caroline could see a tiny trail of footsteps. Her eyes followed the faint prints to a solitary silhouette standing on the narrow footbridge that led to the railway station. It was a woman. She didn't know why, but she was now walking towards her. Caroline felt a strange feeling come over her. Suddenly, a sharp pain in stomach forced her to stop. She gazed at the woman, while she paused to catch her breath. Although it was dark the silhouette seemed familiar. She continued to stare intently. The woman was fairly tall and was wearing a hooded coat. The colour is blue, similar to the one that my mother used to wear, she thought.

Caroline suddenly gasped, 'It can't be.' She closed her eyes and opened them again, 'It is.'

The lady on the bridge stared back at Caroline. Only the sound of the snow settling gently on the ground could be heard.

'It's her,' she gasped. Caroline wanted to call out, but felt the words didn't seem to make it to her lips. Instead, she started to walk slowly towards her. The pain in her stomach worsened with each step. She felt sick and her eyes were struggling to focus. Caroline paused once more, desperately clinging onto the snow covered railings of the bridge. The woman she thought was her stepmother continued to stare back at her. Caroline took another deep breath and used the railing to guide herself once more. It was pointless. The pain grew too intense. Everything around her started to swirl. A loud buzzing noise filled her ears. She stopped, realising that she was slowly losing her balance. The bridge ahead was becoming blurred and the image of the woman started to fade. Suddenly, it all went black.

∽∾∾

She woke to a familiar voice.

'Caroline? Is that you? Are you OK? Come on – let's get you off the cold snow,' a voice said from above.

The icy blanket of snow chilled her back and everything around her was still a little blurred. Someone was holding her. His voice was soft and familiar, but she was still a little disorientated. The numbness in her legs turned to pain.

'What are you doing here?' the concerned voice said.

Caroline was starting to regain consciousness. A very familiar image began to emerge from the dark shadows above.

'Greg is that you?'

Greg said nothing. He did not know why he was there, but he was glad that he was.

It was him – Gregory Earnshaw, the tall handsome blue-eyed boy from her childhood. Yes, it was him – the one that had broken her heart over a year ago, she realised. Suddenly, rage began to well up the lowest depths of her body as painful memories flooded her mind.

'You bastard, what happened to you?'

'Let's not go into that now. I need to get you to a hospital.'

'We were engaged to be married. We were supposed to be meeting at the train station and elope,' she snapped. 'So what happened? Why didn't you show up?'

Greg said nothing. His face looked sad.

As he helped her up she noticed a walking stick propped up against the iron railings. 'You broke my heart and now you show up a week before my wedding.'

Greg looked hurt, but still said nothing. He had recently heard about the imminent marriage. He too, felt a real sense of loss, but also anger. If only she knew, he thought. I understand how it must have looked, but it wasn't like it seemed.

He looked into her fiery green eyes, stroked her Lily white skin and then brushed her blonde hair to reveal, once more, the beauty of her face. He still loved her, but she was someone else's now.

Still weak, she half-heartedly slapped him across the face, but regretted it immediately. Warm tears filled her eyes and soon found their way down her icy-cold cheeks.

He gently wiped them from her face, 'On the way to the station that night I was involved in a fatal car crash. I do not remember much,' he paused.

She glanced at the walking stick she had seen earlier.

'Apparently, the taxi driver had a head-on collision with another vehicle. He and the driver of the other car were killed instantly.' His dark brown eyes looked at her sullenly. 'I miraculously survived and spent nearly nine months in a coma. I am still recovering from the amnesia, but slowly things are coming back to me now.'

She could see the pain in his eyes.

'Only one person knew about our little plan to run away together and get married.'

She remembered it well. She had specifically told him to keep it a complete secret for fear of her stepmother finding out.

'But, why didn't Matthew say anything? He must have known? He was your best friend.' A terrible feeling began to spread over Caroline like a horrible rash.

Greg shrugged his shoulders, 'I told Matthew in confidence about our little plan.' He paused to look into her eyes once more, 'He had also visited me several times in hospital.'

She suddenly remembered the lady on the bridge and quickly glanced over Greg's shoulder, but there was no one on the bridge and the footsteps in the snow had mysteriously disappeared. Caroline had no idea why she had decided to take a walk towards the very train station where Greg and she had planned to meet that night – over a year ago now.

She smiled at him, threw her arms around his neck and kissed him gently on the lips. The moment was theirs.

As he helped her to her feet, she glanced round at the point where she had seen the woman on the bridge.

'Thanks mum', she whispered.

The Menai Strait

Hugh Williams sat shivering. He was looking for any signs of life from the water. He was still in shock. The life raft bobbled on the jostling currents of the Menai Straits. He could see the rescue boat racing to his aid, but they were already too late. Their "Three Peaks Yacht Race" had ended in disaster. It seemed that he had survived and the others had perished. The coveted Daily Telegraph Cup would not be theirs this year, he grimaced. Hugh felt physically sick. The true extent of what had just happened hadn't really sunk in yet.

The RNLI lifeboat drew alongside the tiny life raft. One of the crew threw a strong rope across turbulent water. Hugh just stared at it. He didn't really feel like being saved. Why me, he thought. What have I done to deserve to be saved?

'Come on lad, grab the rope,' shouted one of the rescuers. The two craft rose and fell in synchronisation with the aggressive waves. The skies had darkened as the angry clouds merged. Rain fell sporadically with the availing wind.

The crew didn't wait and soon Hugh felt himself being hauled from the raft and immediately wrapped in a warm blanket. Another search team had joined them and started scanning the area where their vessel had sunk, but it was hopeless. Hugh knew it. The Menai Straits had claimed yet more lives. He rose suddenly arching over the side of the boat. He could no longer hold the fluid that now ejected from his mouth. The lifeboat raced towards the coast where he knew that an ambulance would be waiting for him. He could see the other racers now looking on. In time they would learn about the tragedy. One of the crewmembers tried to comfort him, but he just wanted to be left alone with his thoughts.

He remembered how his lifelong friend Owen Williams had come up with the idea to enter the team for the race. His mind drifted.

The Three peaks yacht race occurs each year and was based on an original idea of the late Bill Tilman. It involved a team comprising; 3 sailors (in their case: Owen Williams, Taff Smallwood and himself) and two runners (in their case: Sally Tissewell and Spike Roberts). Each team had to sail from Barmouth on the Welsh coast, to Fort William in Scotland, via Caernarfon and Whitehaven, climbing to the summits of Snowdon, Scafell Pike and Ben Nevis on the way.

We had trained for months, but nothing could have prepared us for this, he thought. What else could we have done?

'Here, drink this son,' another crew member said, offering him a hot mug of coffee.

Hugh gripped the mug tightly – It was a source of warmth and in a way, offered him some comfort. He took a sip, but it was too hot. The rising steam made his eyes water.

We planned everything so meticulously, he pondered. Achieving a good start to obtain the help of the Menai Straits tidal current after the Snowdon run was the key, he remembered. That's where it all went wrong. The tidal current had dealt them a nasty surprise, one which had proved to be the flaw in their plan and spelt the end for the very talented crew. He attempted another sip from the mug. It felt good. The warm fluid spread hope through his tired body and raised the spirits of his dampened soul. He never realised that coffee could taste this good. At the age of twenty-nine, he was fitter than he had ever been. He had put his 6-foot body through hell and lost nearly a stone in weight. Probably saved my life, he thought.

A crowd had gathered, offering what help they could. Maybe they too have lost love ones in these straits, he thought. Amongst the crowd of on-lookers one face caught his eye as he climbed into the ambulance. It was a lady with dark wavy hair, wrapped in a green full length coat. She smiled at him sympathetically. The paramedics talked non-stop all the way to the hospital, but he said nothing in reply. His thoughts focused on the others out there somewhere and their loved ones. There was a lot heartache to go through before this is all over, he concluded.

∽◦◦∽

Six months later …

Hugh was slowly putting his life back together after the tragedy. The physical scars had healed, but the sleepless nights reminded him of the terrible events that had occurred on that unforgettable day. From the kitchen Hugh heard the familiar thud of the mail hitting the hallway carpet. He quickly scanned through the mail until he came to a hand-written envelope. It was post-marked "Caernarfon." He opened it cautiously, carefully unfolding the beautifully hand-written letter inside.

Dear Mr Williams,

I read about your miraculous survival of the recent tragedy in the Menai Strait and felt duty bound to share some knowledge with you that may or may not be of comfort to, as you continue search for reasons why you were spared. My grandfather too, learnt about the perils of navigating the Menai Strait.

Lemon Zest – Perry A. Simpson

The Menai strait, as you know, is a narrow stretch of shallow tidal water about 14 miles (23 km) long, which separates the island of Anglesey from the mainland of Wales. The differential tides at the two ends of the strait cause very strong currents to flow in both directions through the strait at different times, creating dangerous conditions.

The Menai Strait has another more chilling little secret. It is has one of the oddest coincidences ever recorded, which spans a period of nearly 200 years. This involved three ships that sank in the Menai Strait, just off the coast of Wales:

The first vessel went down on December 5, 1664. All 81 passengers were lost with the exception of one; Hugh Williams.

The second occurred 121 years later, December 5, 1785, where it too, sank in the Menai Strait. Again, all of the passengers perished with the exception of one; Hugh Williams.

Finally, on December 5, 1860, a small 25-passenger vessel sank in the Menai Strait. There was only one survivor – Hugh Williams.

Although, I would agree that three ships sinking in this particular stretch of water on the same date is not earth-shattering, but all the survivors having the same name is a little more than a coincidence – Don't you think?

You are the fourth 'Hugh Williams' to survive a tragedy in this stretch of water!

I hope that this letter finds you in good health and serves to help ease the pain, set your mind at rest and give you hope for the future.

Lemon Zest – Perry A. Simpson

Yours faithfully,

Ethel Williams

(P.S. I have attached some newspaper clippings).

Cojones de Toro

Andrew Pen knew that his work colleague, David Ives, was looking forward to the trip to Madrid with delight. He on the other hand, did not relish the thought of another one of Dave's cuisine nightmares. He remembered their previous disastrous culinary experiences only too well. Some bizarre roasted French game bird it had been in France, he recalled. In Italy it had been, "formaggio marcio", known colloquially as maggot cheese; a unique cheese found in Sardinia and considered a rare delicacy because the locals only eat it when it's filled with thousands of live maggots, he grimaced. The bitter memory almost turned his stomach. Dave had become obsessed by these outrageous cultural delicacies since he heard that the EU was planning to ban such culinary delights. Damn good idea, I'd say. Andy starred at his reflection in the mirror with his dark brown eyes. What the hell has he got planned for us in Spain? He took out his comb a forced it through his thick gingery cropped hair, removed his glasses and inspected them to ensure that they were clean. I must go for an eye test, he thought. Perhaps a brain scan too, he chuckled to himself in an attempt to raise his spirits for the trip.

A last call announcement for British Airways Flight BA0456 to Madrid, bleated out over the rather tired speakers. Time to face Dave, he thought. He wrestled his bag through the double-door arrangement in the main departure hall. Yes, gate 15, I think. He re-checked his boarding card. Dave was waiting impatiently for him at the desk. He stood tall in his smooth blue pinstriped suit; white easy-care shirt, orange tie and matching cufflinks. He was clean-shaven and not a hair was out of place. Andy also noticed that he had topped up his tan with Coppertone and if he wasn't mistaken, he has also touched up his hair colour too.

'Come on Andy, last call went out ages ago,' Dave snapped.

'We've got plenty of time yet.'

They passed swiftly through the final checks and into the business class cabin. Dave took the FT, while Andy settled for the Daily Mail. Business as usual, thought Andy.

'So what's the agenda for today', asked Andy reluctantly.

'Well, the meeting is at 10am, which means we get to leave early and explore the streets of Madrid for Cojones de Torro,' he smiled.

Andy grimaced, I cannot wait. He didn't really want to know, but he knew he was expected to ask, 'What is Cojo de ...?'

'Ah! I am glad you asked me that my dear boy. Cojones de Torro is also known as Criadillas.'

'But what is it?'

'If I am not mistaken, it is in fact Spanish for an animal's testicles.'

'Great,' Andy said despairingly.

'Yes indeed, the eating of the cojones from a freshly slaughtered bull has long been seen as a way of proving ones machismo. For many years now, the Spanish people have flocked to restaurants around the bull rings in the Corrida season to banquet on what they believed to be adrenaline-impregnated flesh of animals they had just seen killed that very day.'

Andy pretended to drift off to sleep.

'Yes indeed, we're in for another culinary treat today my boy.'

⁓⊱⊰⁓

The meeting with the Spanish went as expected, thought Andy. The actual meeting would have only been an hour or so. The rest of the time was made up of "Spanish breaks" – Intervals where the Spanish went for a coffee and discussion in Spanish. He had got used to this meeting style. The meeting was going to spill over into the afternoon and it was agreed to break for a late lunch.

True to form, Dave had managed to negotiate the Spanish into going in search of his plate of criadillas. Juan and Rafael had agreed to take them to some restaurants that would normally serve this now hard-to-find dish. After visiting several restaurants, touring the markets, they eventually ended up at Casa Rodriguez. The smell of greasy fat greeted them as they entered the restaurant bubbling with life. The nicotine-stained terracotta walls were draped with hundreds of pictures of famous Bullfighters. Above the door the mounted head of Barbero stared angrily at the guests. The music could barely be heard over the loud Spanish gathering, reliving past fights of their famous matadors and sipping Manzanilla. They were shown to a table at the rear of the restaurant, where it seemed to be a little quieter.

Andy looked away in horror while Dave insisted on insulting the Spanish waiter with his Anglo-Spanish and kept calling him Manuel.

He has to do it every time.

The mousy-looking little Juan with his standard Mexican-style moustache, crumpled mustard coloured suit and the slick looking, unusually blue-eyed Rafael did not appear to be too phased by Dave's overpowering nature.

Soon the long sought after dish arrived. Dave had described the dish as being baked into a pie, "empanada-style" as he put it, but the dish arrived in chunky gravy, garnished with spicy guindilla chillies and softly fried garlic, served in a rustic earthenware bowl.

Andy delayed the inevitable by raising his glass of red Rioja to toast their Spanish counterparts knowingly.

Dave immediately dived into the dish searching out the meaty organs with his fork, pausing only to take another sip of wine. Onlookers watched on tentatively smiling. Juan and Rafael glanced at Andy, as all eyes now focused on this mad Englishman massacring the famous dish.

Andy on the other hand, was a little more cautious. He had noticed that the normal barnyard taste associated with the soft, almost fluffy, meat had a slight hint of bacon flavour, with an irresistible blend of garlic and chillies overpowering everything.

The waiter folded his arms over his black waistcoat and eyed Dave sourly, 'We don't a get a many foreigners here, senor.'

The waiter speaks English, smirked Andy

'What did you think of our criadillas?'

'Brilliant.' Dave replied stabbing at his teeth with a wooden tooth-pick. 'But, I didn't realise that they'd be so small, once cooked. The ones we saw at Maravillas market today were much bigger,' he added.

'You see senor, those were criadillas de toro,' he paused. 'These are criadillas de cerdo.'

Dave starred at the waiter. Andy suspicions had proved to be correct, pig's testicles.

'Well, sometimes my friend the bull, he wins,' the waiter laughed.

Dave's mouth dropped. He glanced at his plate, then at the others in disbelieve. Then, he rose sharply, quickly pushed his chair back and rushed to the toilet clutching his mouth.

The restaurant erupted into laughter.

Lady on the Road

Martin Pembroke placed his forehead on the steering wheel, pausing so as to catch his breath. His heart raced uncontrollably, sweat oozed from every opening on his bleached face, and his brown eyes were bloodshot. The car had stalled. It was a nice summer's evening, but it felt bitterly cold in the car. Martin really didn't want to get out of the car. He couldn't face the sight of the mutilated body of the beautiful blonde that had just strayed onto the road and under the wheels of his Vectra. The flashback of the sudden sound of the heavy wallop, followed by the crunching thud of her skull on the windscreen, played repeatedly in his troubled mind. It was almost midnight, stair rods of light from the headlights of passing cars, cut pointlessly into the dense fog. Martin tried to compose himself. 'Where's my mobile,' he said fumbling around his feet. During the 30-metre skid it had fallen on the floor around his feet. 'Got it.'

As he sat upright, he realised that the fog had gone and the sky was now filled with a fiery midsummer sunset. He stared at the undamaged windscreen in utter amazement. A rabbit skipped playfully across the road under the thick canopy of trees. In contrast, it felt quite warm now. Martin slowly opened the door, got out and crept slowly round to the front of the car.

Nothing!

He frantically circled the car, looking underneath. Perhaps, she's still alive and has crawled into the undergrowth, he thought. Panicking now, he eagerly searched the surrounding shrubbery.

Nothing!

The only sign of damage, was an array of old scars, cuts and divots in the bark on an old oak tree on the bend ahead. He glanced at his mobile and thought about calling the police, but what could I say? I'd like to report an accident, only it's disappeared. As he walked back to his car he noticed, that the skid marks too, had disappeared.

❦

About three miles on from the scene of the incident, over the brow of a hill, the Hunter's Lodge public house appeared. Martin decided that he would risk a pint. Being a travelling salesman, he never normally drank when he was driving, but the events earlier that evening had severely challenged his judgment. His best explanation was that he must have fallen asleep and dreamt the whole thing. A gentle whisper of smoke rose from the chimney of the redbrick building. As he opened the Georgian-style door, he was greeted by the curious stares of only a handful of locals occupying seats adjacent to the bar. The smell of bacon dominated the air. The mustard-coloured walls displayed the successes of past hunts, together with a rare selection of pictures of hunters, guns and their dogs. The low oak beams looked tired after several hundred years of bracing the uneven ceiling.

'What's up with you me lad. You look like you seen a ghost,' said the big round bearded barman.

Martin managed a smile as he noticed the buttons of the barman's blue chequered shirt struggling to hold his belly in.

'Lager, please,' Martin replied.

'Pint?'

'Please.'

'You're not from round these parts,' he declared.

'No, just passing through.' His hand shook uncontrollably as he raised the glass to his lips.

'You sure you're alright me lad?'

'No, not really – I thought I had hit a blonde lady 3 miles up the road.'

'Oh, what did she look like,' asked an elderly gentleman sat at the table. The slate-grey eyes of his ruby-red chubby face focused intently on Martin.

'Well, she was blonde, wearing a blue dress and I think white shoes. It all happened so quickly. I didn't really get a good look at her. Is she from round here then?'

'Was,' the barman replied abruptly.

Whispers spread amongst the others at the table.

'It be Marian May, daughter of the local priest. She was killed on that very road, probably at the same bend where your car left the road.' He paused. 'In fact, exactly five years ago today,' said the ruby-faced hunter.

Martin looked at his mobile – "Friday September 13th, 1996." A cold chill edged slowly down his spine. He hadn't realised what day it was. It had been such a successful day, that all he could think of was getting home to celebrate.

'That particular bend had been a notorious accident black spot for many a year.'

'Several lives have been claimed by the deceiving nature of that bend,' the barman said brashly.

The marks on the oak tree, Martin remembered.

'Since that fateful day, there has not been a single fatal accident for five years now,' the hunter added, his eyes glaring at him menacingly.

'Some say, that she walks the road in order to prevent any further deaths, but others believe she's waiting for the one that did it,' the barman butted in.

'What do you mean the one that did it?' Martin asked curiously.

'The damn driver that run her down, didn't stop you see,' shouted the hunter.

'The folk round here, believe it were a local lad – John Melcher be his name,' exclaimed the barman.

Martin glared at the old lady at the adjacent table, the hatred in her eyes made him feel uneasy.

'But nobody could prove it see,' added the Hunter.

'He soon moved away after the inquiry,' the barman continued.

'He weren't welcome round these parts no more,' the old lady finally added.

'Folk round here say that poor old Marian will not rest in peace until she gets her revenge,' the hunter gestured.

'And, until that day she continues to wait,' the elderly gentlemen said bitterly.

'Some even say that the next fatal accident to occur on that very road will be that of John Melcher,' the barman speculated.

'He'll die on that bend and Marian will have her revenge,' the old lady chuckled.

'See me boy, our young Marian saved your life tonight – Just like all the others before you,' the barman concluded.

There was an uneasy silence as all eyes focused on a picture on the wall behind the bar.

Martin didn't know quite what to say. The evening had already been bizarre enough, the coincidences too coincidental. He followed their gaze, it's her.

A brown-framed picture of the blonde-haired Marian, wearing the same blue dress and white shoes, hung unevenly on the wall behind the bar.

The picture suddenly fell to floor with a crash. The glass showered the uneven stone floor.

Everybody jumped.

The room fell silent. In the distance the sound of urgent sirens cut through the air. Everyone smiled knowingly, as blue flashing lights raced past the window for the first time in five years.

Emily Rae

The hospital trolley charged through the double doors. 'Clear the way,' shouted the stout staff nurse.

The medical team moved swiftly through the corridors of the hospital and into a private ward. Emily Rae coiled herself up – It seemed to ease the pain. Sweat leaked from every source of the sixty-four-year olds' skin, her eyes watering with the each sharp jolt in her abdomen.

'Can you describe the pain for us Emily?'

'What sort of bloody question is that,' she screamed. She rolled over so that she could face the staff nurse. She glanced at her bleached face, shallow green eyes, and untidy brown shoulder length hair. 'I didn't pay all this money for private medical care to diagnose myself,' she blurted out between the spasms of pain.

The nurse just smiled sympathetically. The young nurse had become accustomed to comments of this nature from private patients. 'Doctor Meadows will be along to see you shortly. In the meantime, I will take care of this cut for you,' the nurse said looking at her left knee.

⁓

A blue fiesta, containing three elderly ladies, Ethel, Beryl and Janet, pulled out of the driveway of 105 Hill Crescent. They had long been friends of Emily Rae and had just heard the news from a neighbour.

'What happened?' Beryl asked looking at the others using her rear view mirror. Janet was sat next to her in the passenger seat.

'Silly old bugger fell off her mountain bike,' replied Ethel, the younger looking of the three with fewer grey hairs and fairer skin complexion.

'Well, I warned her,' Beryl went on.

'Let her be – She's happier since Bernard passed away,' Janet interrupted, adjusting her greying auburn hair in the passenger mirror.

'Well, I'm not so sure. She seems to be on some sort of death wish if you ask me.'

'How do you mean?' asked Janet.

'Well, look at these crazy adventure holidays she's been on,' Beryl replied, swerving the little car into the high street. 'Climbing mountains in the Himalayas, trekking in the Grand Canyon, white water rafting in Scotland, just to name a few.'

Beryl took another left at the lights. 'Then there was paragliding, hang gliding, yachting, balloon riding in the desert,' she added.

'Where ever did she get the ideas?' asked Janet.

'Search me,' Beryl sighed.

'Perhaps, she's just doing all those things she could never have done when Bernard was alive,' offered Ethel. 'She did alright by him, you know.'

'Poor old bugger, I bet he's turning in his grave now,' laughed Beryl.

'What about bungee jumping?' asked Janet.

'She wanted to do that too, but she was worried that her teeth would fall out,' Beryl replied. 'Believe me it was on the list.'

'Yeah, she's a bit accident prone,' Janet gestured.

'Don't,' Beryl laughed. 'Remember the blue mascara?'

They all started laughing.

'She didn't realise till after she got back home from church you know,' Ethel butted in.

Beryl and Janet just looked at each other and then at poor Ethel knowingly.

'Do you remember the vacuum cleaner saga?' asked Janet.

'Do I? I remember it as if it was yesterday,' Beryl scowled. 'What was she using?'

'Plastic bread bags, wasn't it?' Ethel interrupted.

'She told the nice service man that the vacuum cleaner seemed hotter than normal. Do you remember Janet?'

'Yes, the silly bugger nearly burnt the house down,' Janet replied, shaking her head.

'Got a new carpet out of it though,' Ethel pointed out.

'Yes, but the poor guy had no chance – she removed the plastic bag each time he came,' snapped Beryl. 'It was only when the bag finally melted, that he discovered the root cause of the problem – Emily.'

'He was ever so nice about it though,' Ethel added.

'Is she still putting silly things in the fridge?' Janet asked.

'More than likely,' Beryl answered. 'Now she's eating these strange concoctions.'

'Really?'

'Yes. The other day she ate wholemeal bread sandwiches filled with spam, jam and peanut butter, and then wondered why she spent the next two days hovering over the toilet.'

Janet started to laugh, 'Do you know what they call her in the village now?'

'No, go on frighten me,' said Beryl.

'Super-Granny,' interrupted Ethel.

'And do you know why,' she snarled back at Ethel.

'Yes, as a matter fact I do,' she replied with a touch of sarcasm. 'She had sex with that 20-year old student lodger of hers.'

Beryl momentarily lost control of the car, mounted the pavement as she entered the hospital gate, causing some pedestrians to scatter in all directions. She carelessly threw the car into the nearest parking space.

'She what?' Beryl and Janet asked.

'She told me that she had had real sex with her lodger.'

Beryl was too shocked to comment. The very thought just made her feel quite queasy.

'When was this?' inquired Janet.

'A couple of months back.'

'Is that why he left at such short notice?'

'Yes. Apparently, he couldn't cope. She drained him dry I think she said.'

'Well I never ...,' uttered Beryl. 'She's a ...' Beryl couldn't complete the sentence.

'Come on, let's see what the silly sod has gone and done now,' Ethel insisted, taking control. The thought that she knew something they didn't know was very satisfying indeed.

∽ის∾

The three ladies waddled into the reception area to inquire about the fate of Emily. They were told she had undergone a very tricky operation. The operation had gone well and although she was still recovering, they could see her for just five minutes.

'It's Charlie's angels,' Emily joked as the three ladies burst through the door.

The private room had tastefully lilac coloured walls, and was bright and airy. By the side of her bed was a vase of fresh flowers, a glass of water and an extreme sports magazine.

'So, what happened to you,' Beryl asked, resuming control once more. 'I told you about riding that mountain bike.'

'Beryl, give it a rest,' Ethel scowled.

'Well, I fell off the mountain bike, yes, but that's not the reason I had the operation.'

The three ladies listened intently.

'I was suffering from acute abdominal pains. The doctors were convinced it was gall stones or appendicitis. All the tests they did were negative. They then decided to give me an x-ray.'

'And.' Beryl urged.

'Apparently the X-ray showed that I was still carrying a small skeleton of a foetus which they think I must have conceived some years ago.'

Beryl, Janet and Ethel looked at each other in disbelieve, 'You're joking?'

'Somehow, it had become lodged outside my womb and was never expelled from my body.'

'Well, I never,' uttered Beryl.

'Bernard always said that he would leave something special to remember him by,' laughed Emily.

The Receptionist

'Amanda, I have to make a very important phone call to Jonathan Meadows. Can you get him on the phone for me?' Mark asked impatiently. He was still trying to remain calm. 'The number is at the top of this invoice,' he added, handing her the yellow copy. 'As soon as you get through, can you please put the call through to me,' he said assertively. Mark walked towards his office door and turned to face Amanda, 'The survival of this company depends on the payment of that invoice,' he concluded.

'Yes Mr Bloomsbury, I will do it right away.'

If only I believed you, he thought, as he closed his office door.

Bloomsbury & Sons was a small engineering firm located in the heart of the Kent countryside. Mark had taken over the company and literally raised it from closure, transforming it into a very well respected company. He had successfully attained ISO9001 accreditation, and with it came orders from the more prestigious companies. His focus on quality had paid off.

"Boy, it's just a license to print money," his father had said. He did not embrace the Crosby ethos, "Quality costs nothing." The failure to shift with the times had almost killed the seventy-five year-old family firm. However, as the orders grew, so did the debt from the borrowing. Inevitably, the company was now facing mounting cash flow problems. Things were so bad that he was now considering possible candidates for redundancy, from his fifty-strong workforce. Unless he received payment from some of the outstanding invoices in the next few days, he would have no choice. The invoice he had handed to Amanda would be enough to avert the need to make anyone redundant.

Amanda tried the number immediately, but it was engaged. The spring time sun was now strong enough to penetrate the dirty skylights of the small engineering business unit, placing weak spotlights on the small dedicated workforce manning the royal-blue coloured machinery. Amanda had joined the company a month ago and was still working through her probationary period. She had hoped that this would be a fresh start for her. Amanda was a tall, leggy, blue-eyed blonde. She had now grown tired of the blonde jokes and usual clichés.

She tried the number again. 'Engaged again,' she remarked. They must owe a lot of people money, she thought. She picked up the little red watering can and flooded the spider plant that draped itself over the edge of her mucky green filing cabinet.

The noise level rose and fell as the door opened. 'Amanda, we need some more of these,' a bald headed John Farrow said, handing her a grease-stained empty polythene packet. 'They are 8mm brass x 75mm bolts,' he added, pointing to an oily label containing the relevant part number.

'Leave it with me John,' she smiled.

'Did you here the one about the redhead?' John asked.

Amanda, liked John and knew it was best to pacify him, 'No.'

John balanced himself on the corner of her desk.

Lemon Zest – Perry A. Simpson

John proceeded to tell her the joke.

A gorgeous young redhead goes into the doctor's office and said that her body hurt wherever she touched it.

"Impossible!" says the doctor, "Show me."

The redhead took her finger, pushed on her left shoulder and screamed, then, she pushed her elbow and screamed even more. She continued touching different parts of her body and she screamed out in pain each time.

"Well, what do you think it is Doctor?" She asked.

The doctor smiled and said, "You're not really a redhead, are you?"

"Well actually, no" she replied, "I'm a natural blonde – how did you know?"

"I thought as much," said the doctor. "Your finger is broken."

❦

John broke out into uncontrollable laugher. Amanda didn't really find it funny, but continued to pacify him with a false smile. In fact it hit a nerve. Amanda had, on many occasions, thought about dyeing her hair another colour.

'Haven't you got work to do John?' snapped Mark as he opened the door.

'Yes, I'm just on my way Mr Bloomsbury.' 'Amanda.'

'Yes.'

'Do not forget those parts will you, love?'

'Consider it done.'

The noise level rose and fell again as John left the office.

'What happened to my call Amanda?'

'I've been trying all morning, but every time I dial, the number appears to be engaged.'

'Keep trying will you? I must speak to Jonathan Meadows today. We need that payment,' he insisted.

The metal door slammed closed behind him.

Amanda tried the number again. 'Engaged again,' she remarked. I wonder if their telephone line is faulty, she thought. She could tell by the tension in Mark's voice that the call was important. He had been very irritable these past few days, she thought. Just keep trying to get through I guess, she concluded. She processed the paperwork for John's urgent parts and they duly arrived in the early part of the afternoon. The rest of the day seemed to fly by and "clocking out time" was approaching.

Dark clouds flooded the sky, casting a gloomy atmosphere over the workshop. The fluorescent lighting only provided modest coverage. Soon the end-of-day horn sounded and the noise suddenly wound down as the machines were switched off. Within minutes, a sea of workers, dressed in green overalls, were punching their timecards. Their grim faces and silence at the start of the day had now been replaced with smiling and jovial mayhem at the end of the shift.

Suddenly a very angry looking Mark burst through the door. 'What happened to my phone call?' he snapped. He snatched the invoice from her hand.

'I have been trying all day Mr. Bloomsbury, but the line is always engaged.' 'I even contacted BT and ask them to do a line check and ...'

'What number did you dial?' he interrupted.'

'The one on the top of the invoice, like you said.'

'This one?', he asked pointing on the invoice.

'Yes, but...'

'You idiot – that is our number,' he exclaimed. 'No wonder it was engaged.' Unable to contain his rage he threw the invoice at her, 'Get your things and go.'

Amanda slowly gathered her things, tears rolling down her cheeks.

Lemon Zest – Perry A. Simpson

She paused at the door, 'I knew how urgently you needed to speak to Mr. Meadows, so I sent him an email. He sent this via a courier.'

She handed him a cheque for the full payment of the outstanding invoice, signed by "Jonathan E. Meadows."

Prickly Affair

Steve waited impatiently. The doctor had told him that he would be back in ten minutes. That was over one hour ago. The painkillers were starting to wear off and the panic inside him grew. As he sat inside the little well-lit cubicle, he wondered what sort of sick person would deliberately do this to anyone. He could hear voices, of the largely Indian staff, and wondered if he might be their source of amusement.

It was the end of week three and Steve had come to Dubai in the hope of making a fresh start in his life. He had come through an extremely messy divorce settlement that had left him without a home, car and bitter memories. He really thought that he had fallen on his feet when he landed the contract in Dubai, but now, after only three weeks, he knew differently.

He remembered oh so well, his joyous feelings as he arrived at Dubai International Airport, then the welcoming heat and humidity as the automatic doors opened at the exit from the arrivals building. The chaos that followed after that was 'Dubai'. It had proved to be the most frustrating experience of his life. The cultural differences were far greater than he had imagined. After 3 weeks of adaptation to the climate, the culture and other quirky things, he had concluded that that old cliché applied to Dubai; "There's the right way, the wrong way and the Dubai way". To Steve, it was a city of misfits, drawn together by the smell of dirty money.

∽

It was the weekend again and this Wednesday he had decided to try another English pub, the "Old Vic." To his surprise the bar was almost English in its style and décor. He found a high stool at the bar that offered a good view of both the small stage and the large TV screen. The poorly lit space was equipped with the usual solid dark wood bar top, brass foot rest and a haphazard arrangement of tables and chairs for those wishing to dine on traditional English cuisine.

'What would you like to drink sir?' asked the slender looking Indian barman. His red and black waistcoat seemed to match nicely with the gloomy surroundings.

'A pint of Guinness,' he replied.

The drink arrived without delay and Steve handed the barman two ten and one five dirham notes, 'Here you are my friend and keep the change.'

The dark murky liquid slid down with ease. It slowly rejuvenated his body, calming down his nerves, till normality seemed to return.

At the far end of the bar, he noticed a young Chinese girl sitting alone. Her skimpy light white knee-length dress caught his eye. Only a small white hand bag and mobile placed on the bar top appeared to accompany her. Her straight shoulder length jet black hair shimmered in the intense light of the spotlights above the bar. She smiled at him. Pleasant smile, he thought to himself. She took an occasional sip from a tall glass and smiled repeatedly. Each smile got more provocative until Steve could not resist the urge to invite her to join him.

'What your name?' she giggled.

'Steve. You?'

'Oh, Liu Liu,' she giggled.

'Do you want another drink?' he asked. He had been warned about the girls in the bars of Dubai, but he really wanted some company right now.

'Orange juice, please,' she replied.

The barman seemed to know the routine and a fresh glass of orange juice appeared without the need for Steve to say anything. They continued talking, awkwardly exchanging the usual information. She wanted to secure her income for the night, while he just wanted to know how much. In the process, he had learnt that she worked in a shop, but her salary barely covered the rent for the apartment, which she shared with two other girls. She was married, but her husband had been killed in a car crash. Her son, who was barely 6 months old, lived with her mother in Beijing, while she came to Dubai to find work. She had been promised a job and free accommodation in a Chinese 'mafia' house. In reality, she had no money to send home, no money for the next 3-month visa and no money for a flight home. Steve had to admit that her situation was pretty grim and their situations somehow poetically complimented each other.

The noise level rose as the bar began to fill with expats anticipating a premiership classic between Manchester United and Chelsea. The beer was flowing as the crowd jostled and jeered. The room became filled with a smoky haze. Steve found himself shouting rather than talking. She offered an all-night Chinese massage for DHS 500. He agreed and they left.

He remembered the excitement he felt as they sat in the backseat of the taxi. She gripped his arm and placed her head on his bicep. Their clothes left a trail from the door to the bed and he remembered how she practically screamed as he penetrated deep inside her. Her petit breasts barely rose from the surface of her chest, nipples very pert and inviting. Soon their bodies rose and fell until – he felt a stabbing sensation followed by the most excruciating pain imaginable.

ের

The swish of the curtain opening startled him. A grey-haired Dr Irham stepped in, followed by a small Filipino nurse. His tired brown eyes looked at Steve's injuries. 'I am not sure if stitches will help,' he muttered, gazing at his injuries over the top of his very slim glasses. 'You see here,' he pointed. 'These are just puncture wounds and they will probable heal without the need of any form of support. I will get the nurse to clean it and dress it for you,' he said looking at the nurse. 'You'll need pain killers for the next 2 – 3 days and I strongly advise an aids test,' he concluded.

'What caused it?' Steve asked, now fighting back his tears.

'It appears that the young lady had surgery during the birth of her recent son. Somehow, a surgical needle was left inside her,' he smiled.

Chance

'Yes,' Peter shouted at the top of his voice. He leapt to his feet, punching the air with joy. He could not control his emotions and he naturally received some concerned looks from his work colleagues. He fumbled in his desk for his keys. Panic had now taken control. 'Where are my keys?' he snapped, haphazardly working his way through each individual drawer of the 3 draw-unit. In the middle of the busy office, he was now encapsulated in his own little world. The irritating clicking noise from the keyboards seemed to be so distant and the complex maze of desks and light blue partitions simply a blur now. The keys were in my pocket all the time, he sighed. Peter hit the 'off' button on the computer. No time for the controlled shut down, he thought. He had been waiting for this moment for nine months. The clock was ticking faster than ever now and he had no intention of missing the birth of his first child.

Peter Frederick Chance was in his late-forties, with the usual invasion of grey hairs on his scalp, blending with his naturally light brown hair, to give him that mature and distinguished look. His deep ocean blue eyes had been an alluring magnet to the opposite sex, but after all these years, he had finally found the girl of his dreams. This time he had found true love. The nightmares and painful memories of his first love affair were melting away.

∽∘∾

Peter was in the car heading for the hospital. He weaved the silver Ford Focus in and out of the traffic, willing the traffic to clear. 'Come on – Move it idiot,' he shouted. His eyes had darkened and now his greatest fear had been realised – an accident ahead.

The traffic ground to a halt and now his panic turned to rage. He thumped the steering wheel repeatedly, 'Why me, for heaven's sake?' He yanked the handbrake and slapped the dashboard. His nerves were in tatters, so close, yet so bloody far, he sighed. This is turning into a nightmare. His mind started to regurgitate his past and he thought once more about Elena Dickinson. They had met and immediately fell in love at the local village disco. Their relationship flourished until she had fallen pregnant. It was the first of many shocks to come. Why hasn't the pain gone away? he thought. Why can't I simply move on? he grimaced. Nicole is so different in many ways. Maybe things will change when this new baby arrives, he concluded.

Blue flashing lights and the sounds of sirens approached from behind. First the police car, followed shortly by the ambulance. The pulsing of the blue lights made him think hard and realise how stupid he had just been. Driving too fast had never got me anywhere any quicker, only increased the risk of me too, having an accident. He turned on the radio and tried to relax. The tune seemed familiar. It was their song and yet another painful reminder of what could have been.

'Why did she not try to contact me?' he asked. He was gutted when her parents sent her away, but even more disappointed that she hadn't made any attempt to make contact with him. Her parents never liked me, he scowled. I wasn't of their class, he laughed. They were stinking rich and he was just a peasant in a suit. They controlled and manipulated poor Elena like a puppet, he thought, as the bitter memories flooded his mind.

He remembered the emptiness he felt inside, the loneliness, the pain of not knowing, the fear of not being there for her and the baby. He hated not seeing their new born, but most of all, he hated not knowing why. He had assumed that she had the baby, but it was of course possible, that she had been forced to abort. The very thought made him shudder and feel quite sick. Yet, he had always hoped that she had their baby.

In the end, the loss proved to be so great that constant illnesses and depression had cost him his job at the bank. For many years, he had notched up more one-night stands than he cared to remember and his best friend was a bottle of 'Jim Beam', which was always available and never let him down – then Nicole came into his life.

Nicole was a tall brunette with tantalising russet coloured eyes, a figure to die for, quick witted, intelligent and a smile that made the cobwebs sparkle. They married, decided to start a family and the past had been slowly fading away, until now.

⸎

The sound of a horn from the vehicle behind brought his thoughts to an abrupt end. The traffic was starting to move again and his adrenaline replaced the ill feeling with determination to be there for Nicole. I am not going to let anything come between me and the birth of this child, he thought.

He veered the car sharply to the right and slipped into the infamous "Cherry Tree Lane". He didn't know why he had decided to take this road, as it was certainly not a route he would normally dream of taking. The overhanging trees cast gloomy shadows over the narrow lane. Wild-looking bushes brushed against the car in places. He wasn't driving very fast, but it seemed as though he was rallying. He juggled with the brakes and gears, as he navigated his way through the assortment of pot holes. Suddenly, the front end of a red car appeared from a side junction. He swerved, mounted the low grass verge, and punched a hole through the high Hawthorne hedge, as the car flew into the newly ploughed field. Glass and mud showered him as the car rolled several times, until the momentum from the impact had ceased.

He felt blood trickle down the side of his head, but had no inclination to move just yet. His mind was still spinning. All he knew at that moment was that he seemed to be still alive.

'Hey, are you OK?'

He stared in utter amazement at the face that appeared in the window. Was he already dead? he thought. He glanced again, at what he thought, was himself. Was he now looking down upon himself? It couldn't be. Is it? Surely not, he pondered.

The young man that helped free him from the wreckage was the spitting image of himself, even the tiny mole on his left cheek was the same, and of course, the matching blue eyes.

'You're bleeding,' he said frantically. 'I'm sorry…, I didn't.'

Peter was unable to say anything. His eyes just scanned the young man that stood before him.

'My name is Simon Dickinson.'

Peter realised now that he wasn't dead. More surprisingly, he also realised, that this complete stranger he had met purely by chance, could only be … Elena's son, my son, our son.

The Perfect Egg

'Mr. Atkins, someone once told me that "Time is free, but it's priceless. You can't own it, but you can use it. You can't keep it, but you can send it. Once you've lost it, you can never get it back."

There was a short pause as they exchanged looks. The grey-haired Mrs. Tate examined his casual attire of jeans, white crumbled shirt and scuffed shoes. Her gaze sharpened when her eyes met with his big bushy beard and out of control frizzy brown hair. She tossed her head and sighed indignantly.

'Please come this way,' Mrs Tate said firmly, handing back his ID card. Tom Atkins followed the sprightly seventy-year old lady into the kitchen where she assertively ushered him to the nearest chair, located at the head of a large oak kitchen table.

'Tea, Mr. Atkins?

'Yes, please.'

'Early Grey, Assam, Darjeeling, Gunpowder ...?'

'Earl Grey will be fine thanks,' he interrupted her.

Tom watched this unconcerned little old grey haired lady intently, as she manoeuvred her way around the kitchen. It was hard to believe, he thought to himself. Tom Atkins introduced himself as a freelance writer and that he had become fascinated by her case, so much so, that he had decided that to come and interview her himself.

'You have 5 minutes and 30 seconds,' she interrupted, turning a large wooden egg timer over and the placing it in front of them on the table. The grains started to filter through the narrow neck into the bottom of the ancient timer.

'Not long. I have so many things that I would like to ask you Mrs Tate,' he replied slightly puzzled by the egg timer.

'Time stays long enough for those who use it wisely Mr Atkins.'

'Albert Einstein?'

'I think you'll find it was Leonardo da Vinci. Was that one of your questions?'

'Err. No,' he replied feeling slightly flustered. 'I'm writing an article for the local Gazette and I wanted to ask you some questions about your missing husband.'

'Well, I didn't think you'd come for the tea Mr. Atkins.'

Tom paused to survey which questions he really needed to ask. 'Do you think the police will ever find your husband?'

'Only if they know where to look Mr Atkins,' she smiled.

Strange answer, he thought. 'So you still think there is a chance of finding him?'

'In a manner of speaking,' she cunningly replied.

She's good, he admitted. No wonder DCI Bridges and his team drew a blank on this case, he thought. Right now Tom felt that there was a thick wall of ice between him and the truth. It was like a game of chess, where his opponent already knew all the moves necessary to end the game.

'Do you have anymore questions for me?', she asked smiling cheekily at him with her slate-grey eyes. Her perfect teeth gleamed in the faint light.

'Why do you think that the police are convinced that you have something to do with the disappearance of your husband?'

'The police have very vivid perceptions about the people of this world. You see Mr. Atkins,' she paused. 'In this world the distinction between the past, present, and future is only a stubbornly persistent illusion.'

Tom knew that somewhere in her answer was a clue that would solve this case, but he just couldn't see it. She is a very clever woman, cool, calculated and above all, in complete control of her emotions, he concluded.

'Mrs Tate, you stand to make a lot of money from the death of your husband.'

'Look Mr Atkins,' she snapped. 'As I told the very charming DCI Bridges, the insurance company are not going to pay out a penny of my claim, unless proof of his death can be provided.'

She has a point, he thought. 'So you haven't put in a claim then?'

'What's the point? No body, no booty as the rappers would say,' she chuckled.

He noticed the more mellow tone in her voice. So if she's not interested in the money, what other motive would she have had? Did the force indeed jump to the wrong conclusion? Tom pondered a moment longer before asking his next question. He glanced at the timer. The pile of grain draining through the narrow gap was less than the pile forming in the bottom half of the timer. He guessed barely three minutes remaining.

'Mrs. Tate, what other possible motive would you have for killing your husband?'

It was a stab in the dark, but she didn't seem surprised by the question. If anything, she seemed to welcome it with a gleeful smile.

'You're not a freelance writer at all are you Mr. Atkins?'

That question came unexpectedly, 'Was it that obvious?'

'No, not really,' she paused. 'Let me guess – DCI Chance I presume?'

She is good; I'll give her that. 'Was it the hair, the beard, the clothes?' he surrendered.

'Come, come now DCI Chance. Don't be too hard on yourself. The little disguise is quite divine. It was merely a process of reasoning. I had read that DCI Bridges had been transferred to another case. It was only a matter of time before I received a visit from the charming young DCI Chance. You've become quite a celebrity with the local press, with your impeccable record. No, you are also too well built to be a journalist,' she laughed.

She's got balls I'll give her that, he sighed.

'To answer your question,' she paused. 'Ron made the most perfect hard-boiled eggs. The day we got married he promised to make me a hard boiled egg for my breakfast everyday.'

DCI Chance listened intently. He had no idea where this was leading, but she was almost definitely in control of each move.

'It would be terrible to lose someone who kept a promise like that all these years, don't you think detective?'

He smiled curiously.

'So, one must preserve a quality like that in some way, don't you think detective?'

DCI Chance had no idea what she was talking about.

He just assumed it be another one of her cryptic clues.

The last grain had drained into the bottom half of the timer.

They both glanced at the timer.

It was then that a grizzly thought suddenly popped into his head. He grabbed the timer and examined the contents very carefully through the curved glass.

'Rather ingenious don't you think detective?'

'Perfect,' he replied, rotating the remains around in the glass.

The Wall

Sandra woke suddenly. It was only a dream, but always the same dream, she thought. Sweat trickled down her spine, as she sat bolt upright in the bed. John was sound asleep. She reached across to the cluttered pine sideboard and took a sip of water from a tall glass. She felt a calming sensation spread through her body as the water flowed down to her stomach. Outside the light from the full moon placed a large shadowy spotlight on the damp lawn. Sandra, wide-awake now, turned on her bedside light and fumbled for her book. Only the turning of the pages and the occasional hoot of an owl broke the silence. John lay motionless. How can he sleep in this mess? She thought, glancing around the partly decorated room. Since they embarked on the renovation work, their room had become a store for tools, materials and anything else that might be needed at a later date. She had to admit, that when John Sparrow starts one of his little 5-minute projects it always results in long-term chaos.

The book started to slide from her grip, crashing to the floor. Sandra jumped as an eerie echo travelled throughout the house. John didn't even flinch.

What was that? she thought. Sandra was convinced that she had heard something downstairs. There it is again. She listened more intently. It's coming from downstairs. She continued to listen, holding her breath so that she had a better chance of identifying the source of the noise. Only the sound of her heart could be heard, as it started to race. The seconds seemed like minutes.

It sounds like someone crying.

She shook John's shoulder. He groaned and turned over to face the opposite wall.

It is definitely someone crying. She rose slowly from the bed, quickly slipped on her skimpy pink dressing gown and matching slippers. No point trying the wake the living dead, she joked looking at John. Sandra crept slowly to the bedroom door, pressed the large brass lever until she could feel that the door was free. She carefully pulled the door steadily towards her, sliding gently through a narrow gap. An ice-cold breeze swept in from the hallway. Goose pimples quickly erupted all over her body. It was very dark. Only the faint beams of light from the moon guided her as she tiptoed along the wooden floor towards the top of the staircase.

There was a sudden crack that echoed around the empty hallway.

Sandra's stomach rumbled, momentarily causing a tickling sensation in the back of her throat. Her heart missed several beats. 'That damn mousetrap,' she gasped. She paused to compose herself at the top of the stairs. Warm air drifted up the long flight of freshly varnished wooden stairs, accompanied by the stale smell of onions and garlic. The crying appeared to have stopped.

Placing her hand on the ornate carved wooden rail, she carefully placed her foot on each step, one-by-one, as she worked her way down into the dark hall below. Only the irregular creeks from the century old link between the two levels disturbed the deadly sound of night. The air temperature plummeted, as she descended to the bottom of the staircase.

The crying had started again. It's coming from the lounge. A tiny shock wave ripped through her body as she realised that this was exactly like her dream. Her breath, chilled by the night air, formed a dense mist as she exhaled. Curiosity took control. Just as in her dream, Sandra felt herself being drawn into the lounge by some strange force of nature.

She gasped, as she approached the lounge door, an icy blast of air engulfed her as she stood at the door. Just as in her dream, a little old lady stood facing the wall. The image in real life was clearer, but the colours of her clothing were bleached. Sandra seemed unperturbed and observed the movements of the mystery lady. Her clothes look very old, possibly Georgian, she thought. She continued to watch her as she paced up and down the wall, sobbing profusely, soaking up the tears with the bottom of her frilly white apron.

'Just as my dream,' she whispered.

'What are you doing down here?'

Her heart stopped, as she turned.

'God John, what are you trying to do? Give me a heart attack?'

The air temperature rose sharply and the image of the little old lady suddenly disappeared. Sandra felt a sudden blunt pain in her stomach. The moon resumed its presence through the adjoining window.

Sandra stomped back up the stairs, 'I heard a noise.'

'You should have woken me.'

'Huh, I tried.'

'Oh.'

They climbed back into the four-poster bed, adjusted the covers and soon they both drifted off to sleep.

∽⦾⦽∽

The entire house was suddenly shaken by an almighty thump. Sandra found herself falling. The pain of the impact quickly replaced the strange sensation of weightlessness, as they crashed onto the ground below.

Clouds of dust engulfed them. Not sure what to do, they both lay very still. Rubble surrounded the remains of the bed.

'What the hell have you done John?' It was the first thing that popped into her mind. 'I told you that this project was far too adventurous this time.'

'Well, you got your way in the end,' he cheekily replied, pointing at the pile of rubble where the lounge wall had once stood.

Two strong beams of light tore through the swirling plumes of dust. The wreckage of a large lorry occupied the lounge. The motionless body of the driver was slumped through the windscreen – dead. On the ground beside them, Sandra could see the remains of another body. As the dust cleared she could see the remains of a clothed skeleton of what appeared to be, a little old woman, dressed in a blue dress, and frilly white apron.

'It can't be,' she gasped.

'What are you blabbering on about?' John coughed.

'It's the little old lady from my dream.'

John was still dazed and had no idea what Sandra was talking about. 'What little old lady?'

'That little old lady,' she continued pointing to the fragile remains. 'Her constant crying woke me earlier. I couldn't sleep and in the end I came down to investigate. Remember? You startled me'

John scowled at her in despair, as he started to remove the rubble from his legs.

'I wonder who she is. Poor thing, she must have been buried in that wall all these years.'

'She probably complained about the mess during the last renovation,' John joked.

The Bonfire

Dave, remember to make sure you burn everything and I mean everything. You understand?'

'Yes, Mr Brown,' Dave scoffed. What does he take me for? Dave grimaced. He knows that I always get the job done, he huffed.

Jason Brown was now the sole proprietor of a very successful investment company, who specialised in a number of, lucratively managed fund portfolios. He had successfully rid himself of three troublesome partners and since then, the money flowed like water through the firm's accounts. However, due to some business irregularities, the Inland Revenue was now investigating the firm. This meant that the company records were in need of a slight adjustment. Jason knew it was only a matter of time before the police joined in the hunt for the alleged missing funds.

Jason had known Dave since the day he knocked on his front door asking for a job. Dave Stokes was in his late thirties, around six-feet tall, mousy build, and balding slightly. He was also a bit of a practical joker and had an extremely annoying horsy laugh. Dave had had a turbulent working career and never managed to hold a job for more than six months. Although he was educationally challenged, Dave was generally reliable and he had managed to remain under the employment of Mr Brown for nearly three years now.

Jason felt confident that he could rely on Dave to burn some unwanted records. 'Good night Dave, see you in the morning.' He paused and momentarily turned to face Dave. 'Any problems call me.'

'Sure Mr Brown.'

Jason quickly opened the door of the BMW. Sitting in the driver's seat, he stared with pride at the sign hanging above the entrance of the main gate. Well, this should keep the wolves of authority off my back, he thought. He reluctantly started the car and put it in drive. The car crept slowly forward and then sent tiny stones flying across the forecourt, as he accelerated out of the gate.

Dave was not at all happy. Football was the only real love in Dave's life and tonight was the meeting of two European giants: Real Madrid versus AC Milan. He was going to miss it. Glancing at the massive piles of folders, he knew that there was no way he could possibly burn all this lot in time for the start of the match. I will have to improvise, he thought.

It was a mild evening, a few greyish clouds in the sky were being helped along by a slight easterly breeze. The thick smoke started to spiral as Dave lit the first pile of papers in the large metal container. Soon orange flames rose high into the sky, throwing pieces of charcoaled remains into the air. Dave sat on an old white patio chair and constantly fed the hungry fire. Now and again, he would poke the ashes with a disused broom handle to ensure that every piece had been burnt. As he did so, large plumes of smoke rose into the air, together with a flurry of charcoaled paper, each fringed with an orange glow.

In between feeds, he had rigged up the radio through an adjacent office window, so that he could at least listen to the match. There was a roar as soon as he tuned into the correct channel. AC Milan had taken an early lead. 'Damn, I knew this was going to be a good match,' he groaned. The excitement grew as Real Madrid equalised two minutes later. Dave knew that he was missing an epic.

I have got to try and finish this lot before half time, he thought. Possible, he continued, as a sudden thought hit him. It was risky, but worth it, he smiled.

Orange flames roared from the container as Dave sprayed petrol onto the next pile of paper to be burnt and then threw it into in the fire. The flames engulfed the entire metal container, down the sides and onto the grass, following the trail of petrol. He frantically stamped on the burning grass to extinguish the flames. Then the hem of one of the legs of his overalls caught fire. He rolled around on the grass like a play-acting Italian footballer, trying to secure a penalty from the referee. He finally freed himself from the blazing overalls. It was an Oscar-winning performance. That was close, he sighed.

A sudden gust of wind started to blow loose pages across the grass and onto the fence. Sweat poured down Dave's face as he ran back and forth chasing to retrieve each loose page.

It had been a close thing, but he did manage to burn all the paper in time for him to make the second half. Feeling disappointed that there were no more goals the remainder of the game, he took a can of beer from the fridge, and slumped on his chair in front of the television, hoping to catch the goals he had missed on the late news.

He quickly flicked through the channels, paused, and went back one channel. It was the local area news. They showed earlier footage of twenty fire fighters bravely fighting to bring a fire under control. Three business units had been already been destroyed. Nearly two hundred people in nearby houses had to be evacuated from their homes, while the fire brigade fought to prevent the fire spreading further. He watched in a state of shock. It isn't possible, he thought. I dampened the remains with cold water from the hose. There is no way. He turned the volume up. As he listened to the extended report, his beer suddenly lost its flavour.

'What do you think caused the blaze?' asked the reporter.

'We have only just started our investigation into the cause of the blaze, but it does appear as though the fire may have been caused by an electrical fault in a small portable radio in unit six.'

'Jason Brown's Financial Services?'

'Yes, I believe so.'

The Secret Recipe

'Good morning Mrs Moon, my ... '

'Miss,' she interrupted.

'Good morning Miss Moon, I am Police Constable Steele and I am here in connection with an alleged break in at 25 High Street, Stansted Mill Heath. This is that address and I assume that it was you who raised the alarm?' the tall, uniformed officer said in a very low, but direct tone. His stern brown eyes surveyed her reaction. He took out his little black notebook and turned to a new page.

'It is indeed officer and yes it was me who reported the break in,' she replied looking around at the chaos.

The tall young officer added to his notes and followed her through the glass front door. The lights were on and at first glance it didn't look as though there had been a break in. The arrangements of chairs and equipment seemed to in the same locations where they had been left at the close of business the previous day. The upmarket brand products stored on shelving around the saloon appeared to be undisturbed.

'Was anything actually taken Miss Moon?'

'Well officer, it doesn't look like it,' she hesitated. She had already concluded that this was more than just a burglary.

'I will take a look around Miss Moon if you don't mind,' he said, removing his helmet and placing it on the counter next to the cash register, which he had already noted, hadn't been tampered with. 'Can you please double-check to see if anything has been taken?' The officer added to his notes and started to carefully pick his way round the tiny salon.

'OK, I'll do my best.'

Margaret Moon was in her mid-fifties, but had the complexion and figure of a twenty-year old. Her tight fitting black leggings and white jumper somehow tastily flaunted the natural curvature of her body.

'I see that you are fully booked until the end of April, Miss Moon?'

'Yes, we always have at least one-month waiting list,' she cautiously replied. She ran a very successful beauty salon in the heart of the small market town. 'Business is so good, that I am looking for new premises,' she added. She was attempting to take the chill out of the frosty atmosphere.

PC Steele said nothing, just kept jotting the details down and continued in his search for clues. 'What is it that you actually do here Miss Moon?'

I would have thought that was obvious young man, she thought. But, I guess that being a man he has never stepped inside a women's beauty salon before, she concluded.

'It is a beauty salon for women,' she teased, her glittering green eyes scanned the young officer.

'What does that entail? Miss Moon?'

'We take an ordinary woman from the street and turn her into a super model,' she answered sarcastically.

PC Steele seemed unperturbed and just kept on writing his notes. 'Can you elaborate more for me Miss Moon?'

'Well officer, we artistically style hair, we create a new-look using make-up to disguise those unwanted blemishes on a tired old face, we remove that unwanted hair in those embarrassing places that make a woman feel less than a woman.'

PC Steele remained cool and let the sarcasm wash over him. He had established that there had been a forced entry through an office window. At this stage of his investigation, he concluded that there didn't appear that anything of any value had been taken. So, what was our unwanted intruder looking for, he pondered. 'Do you have anything of value here, Miss Moon?'

'Depends what you mean officer. I don't leave any cash here overnight, if that's what you mean. There is about £2000 of beauty products, that's it,' she replied.

'You don't happen to keep the family jewels here,' he asked, breaking into a smile. I am sure she knows the reason for this break in, but ..., he thought. He meticulously, but carefully inspected the office area. The drawers had been opened and the contents scattered all over the floor. 'It would appear that our intruder was looking for something in this office. You wouldn't happen to know what that might be would you Miss Moon?'

'I have no idea,' she lied. She knew very well what the intruder was looking for, but she also knew that they went home empty handed.

'I notice that about eighty percent of your clients are booked in for waxing, Miss Moon.' He watched her very closely. 'I cannot see any waxing products,' he announced.

He's much smarter than he looks, she concluded. 'The wax I use is an ancient tribal recipe. My grandfather discovered it during a trip to the Brazilian rainforests many years ago.'

'What is so special about your wax recipe?'

'There are a lot of different waxes used for waxing, most of which are manufactured using man-made ingredients,' she paused to open an aluminium case. She handed him a plain glass jar with a silvery tin screw top. 'This wax is completely organic, made only with natural ingredients,' she continued. 'It completely removes the hair, with no signs of redness, no skin irritation and leaves a women's skin extremely smooth and clean,' she added.

'What sort of ingredients?

She pretended not to hear.

He removed the steel lid, 'Weird smell,' PC Steele pointed out.

'Natural solutions rarely smell or taste that nice officer.'

He dabbed his finger in the sticky yellow paste. It tastes bitter and has a sort of tired musky smell, he observed.

If only he knew, Miss Moon grimaced.

'So, it could be that your intruder was searching for some of your wax or maybe, the secret recipe Miss Moon?'

'Yes, it is possible.' She knew only too well what her intruder was looking for.

'Do you know who might have been responsible Miss Moon?'

'No idea, officer,' she lied. Miss Moon knew who was behind it.

'Well Miss Moon that concludes my inquiries for the moment.' Should you think of anything that might help us with our investigation, please give me a call on this number and ask for PC Ian Steele,' he said very formally.

With that, he placed his little black notebook in his breast pocket, collected his helmet and left without delay, through the front door.

⚬♋⚬

The rapidly falling sun was soon washed away and replaced by the dark night sky. The noise from the traffic outside had steadily died. The staff had fulfilled another very busy waxing schedule. Margaret Moon locked the door, turned out the lights, picked up the large aluminium case and left via a door at the rear of the property. She crossed a small courtyard and then entered another building immediately behind. The door opened into a very dimly lit room – It was ice cold. There she removed several jars from the case and walked across the room to a large marble table. On an adjacent table, there was a large hand carved rosewood coffin, fitted with large brass handles. Margaret very careful and meticulously scraped a brownish coating from the body of a deceased man and deposited the pale yellow greasy paste into one of the jars. As well as the sole proprietor of the beauty salon, Miss Moon was also the proud owner of: "MJ Moons Funeral Directors"

'Mother our secret recipe is safe, at least for the moment,' she smiled.

Silver Fox

The room was cold because of the icy breeze that penetrated the failing double glazed window. The rain echoed Dolores' mood against the windowpane. She had only been married to Eddie for a month and already she was finding it difficult to adapt to married life around his long-standing work pattern. Dolores wanted to settle down to a more rational relationship where work fitted in with their needs.

In their mischievous days it had been fun. He would work the late shift; she would wait patiently for him to come home. His absence always heightened their yearning for each other. The sex varied from tender to adventurous, but was always a voyage of discovery. Starting a family had been discussed on several occasions, but wasn't really on their agenda just yet. Dolores being the main earner and the rapidly rising house prices simply added to their ensuing predicament. Probably explains the sudden caution in our sex life recently, she thought. But, nothing has changed, she countered. According to friends and work colleagues, it already had and would get worse before it got better. A cold shimmer ran through her veins, covering her entire body with goose pimples. The thought of getting too serious about life was quite scary, she thought. Marriage is only a vow and a signature on a piece of paper, she protested. It shouldn't spoil the fun, she insisted.

She carefully retrieved her half-read novel, which was carefully placed facedown on the white duvet. Dolores slowly drifted into the fictional world and assumed the role of the protagonist. 'Why is life so complex?' She whispered. Perplexed, she glanced at the clock. The book wasn't making the time pass any quicker. She slammed the book down, only to pick it up again and read on a bit more, only to put the book down again to wrestle with her thoughts. Dolores recalled how the heroine had just discovered that she was pregnant and her dilemma was who the real father was. She read on. She paused for thought again as she reached the part where the heroin had to decide between announcing that she was pregnant and say nothing about her one-night stand with her boss or getting rid of the baby. Dolores sympathised with the heroin, because she had also had a close call recently. On that occasion, her late period was just a false alarm. The difference here was that Dolores knew that Eddie would have been the father of her child.

Still restless, Dolores wondered when her little silver fox would return. A cheeky smirk washed over her as more tantalising thoughts surfaced. What will he want, straight sex or something a bit more adventurous? she joked. Should I surprise him by dressing up in something a little more provocative? She teased. On top of the bed, in the bed, a knee trembler against the wall, naughtily over the dressing table, a freestanding waltz in the middle of the bedroom floor or sensual pleasure in the shower, she smirked. The list is endless. For three long years they had enjoyed a hot, passionate affair and although she loved Ed so much, his past still left some doubt in their relationship. Confused and afraid, Dolores read on. Within a matter of minutes her eyes blinking slowly closed and she drifted off to sleep once more.

⁓℈⁓

Outside the wind had picked up speed, the temperature had suddenly dropped and hailstones beat down incessantly.

Lemon Zest – Perry A. Simpson

An almighty crack and a long crumbling rumble quickly followed a fiery flash that lit the sky. Dolores had slept right through it and was unaware that the electricity supply had been cut off. Darkness fell heavier than normal, concealing anything that sought refuge in one of the many darkened hideaways.

Dolores woke suddenly, unsure why, but was aware of the presence of something or someone. As she glanced up a flash of lightning lit the room and a silhouette of a man occupied the doorway.

'Come and join me my little silver fox,' she jested, tossing the quilt aside. He hesitated at first, then hurriedly removed his clothing and slid into the warmth under the duvet. It was too dark to see anything, but Dolores could feel the hardness in his groin grow rapidly. Improvise, she decided, pulling her silky knickers to one side as she guided him in deep inside her. God he is really hard, she gasped. He slowly rocked to meet her gently upward movement. Their jaws engaged in a passionate kiss, sending a warm breeze down her spine. Something was different tonight. She couldn't place it, but closed her eyes to absorb the tenderness of the moment. As she ran her arms around his waist, their legs interlocked to form a tight bond. He feels much more tense than usual, she thought. Extremely content with his sensitive touch, it was time to throw caution to the wind. Her grip tightened, pulling him even deeper inside her pining body. Dolores was glad to have the old Eddie back. She had needed this so much and was desperate to savour every sensual twinge inside her. Dolores began to groan uncontrollably. It hasn't been like this for a long time. Dolores let out an appreciative scream. He gasped jubilantly, struggling to regain his breath. She could feel his body jerk uncontrollably as he slowly withdrew. She saw his silhouette disappear, closing the door as he went. He usually gives me little cuddle before taking a shower, she frowned. Dolores didn't really care because all her fears about the demise of the passion in their relationship had been washed away in this recent stormy encounter.

⌒◜◟◝⌒

"Hi darling," a voice called through the bedroom door. Dolores stirred, raising her right arm to protect her eyes from the bright light.

'You took your time,' she muttered.

'The storm blew down some trees on the main road. All the traffic had been diverted through Staunton,' he explained.

Still not fully awake Dolores had no idea what the hell he was talking about.

'But now your Silver Fox is here. Have you been asleep long?'

Dolores gazed up at the ceiling, not sure whether she was dreaming this conversation. She was really confused. Had all this been a dream? She thought. As she propped herself up, she felt that tell-tail damp patch on the sheet beneath her. There was no mistake. Couldn't have been a dream, she panicked. The soreness and discomfort confirmed her fears. An ice-cold chill suddenly washed over her body, the hairs on the back of her neck stiffened and beads of sweat cleansed her brow. The repulsive thought that had been sown deep in her soul had flourished into an unwelcome reality.

Aqua Massage

Despite all her various phobias, Maureen Stanton had just made a very bold decision indeed. She had convinced herself to try an "Aqua Massage."

Maureen was a round large woman weighing over 200kg and always wore jeans and a large baggy sweatshirt. Her low self-esteem had plagued her since that little incident at primary school. For most of her life, she had hated herself and her body. Despite all the various therapies and treatments, she was still frightened to visit busy places. Public places, such as hospitals, clinics, etc., still made her feel very uncomfortable. Being very self-conscious she had tried various diets. At best, some worked while she was on the diet, others simply made her ill. She even considered taking up yoga classes, but because of her fear of crowds, she could attend one-to-one tuition with a qualified instructor, but this proved to be far too expensive. More recently, she had read about this revolutionary new massage technique in several magazines and had also visited the various web sites.

Maureen took out a blue folder from her desk to review her collection of brochures. Each key page was meticulously labelled with a little yellow numbered post-it note. An A4 sheet of paper summarised the key information for the purpose of quick referencing.

The literature bragged, "Using our proven technology, you can now offer your clients the same health benefits of a traditional hour-long massage in only 15 minutes." Sounds promising, she had thought. After more in depth research, Maureen learnt that, "The client remains clothed and dry for privacy and comfort, with no post-session clean-up of oils or contaminated water." Perfect, she thought. No need to remove any of my clothing, no need to shower, so good for her dermatitis.

She continued to work down her list. "The spray bar travels in such a way that it is possible to, either the massaging the full length of the body, or simply select a specific area to concentrate on." She nodded in approval. Work on areas such as my bum, stomach and ...

Next entry that had caught her attention read, "The water jets simulate a fingertip massage. The force can be adjusted to suit the sensitivity of the client with a consistency that cannot be so easily achieved by the conventional manual massage." Another good point, she admitted. Oh, a massage without the need for anyone to touch my body, she smiled, feeling much more positive.

She continued to read, "The pulsating water jets can be set from a relaxing 2 cycles per second up to a revitalizing 10 cycles per second. This can be varied independent of water pressure for maximum benefit and client sensitivity." Too technical, but sounds important, she remarked.

After working down the list she came to the final point, "The water temperature can be set between 90°F to 104°F using the ergonomically-styled electronic thermostat. She smiled, as she placed the folder into her bag.

However, it wasn't just the many favourable features of the aqua massage that helped her to make, what she believed, would be a life changing decision. A local clinic in the town specialised in Aqua Massage, "offering private suites for ultimate privacy", the advert claimed. This meant that she could book a private suite and that she would not even have to worry about sharing a crowded waiting room. The service came with a five-minute instruction period and then she would have no need for any further assistance. Absolutely perfect, she smiled, picking up her brown bag, coat and scarf and left.

༄

Maureen was punctual arriving on time, so as not to have to wait in the reception. The small clinic was located in a quiet cul-de-sac, just off Bank Street. This area was famous for its specialists and niche well-being organisations. There were no large ugly banners above the doors, only solitary solid brass plaques. Maureen's heart began to race. She paused, 'I must do this. I want to do this.'

She braced herself, opened the door, and entered.

A stout-looking, dark-haired woman, wearing a white coat smiled politely at Maureen. She quickly rose from her seat at the small, modern-looking reception desk. 'Good afternoon, Miss Stanton.' Her soft green eyes offered a warm welcome. According to the badge on her lapel, her name was Eva.

'Good afternoon,' Maureen mumbled.

'Would you like to follow me? I'll show you to your suite.'

Maureen reluctantly followed the tall thin lady.

She swiftly led Maureen through a white panelled door and into the moderate-size suite. It was bright, airy and clean. The walls had a hint of blue and Maureen immediately felt relaxed by the presence of a nice calming aura.

'It's much bigger than I imagined,' Maureen said. In fact, it not all like the pictures, she thought. She was feeling a little uneasy

'It's the latest model from Germany. It's the best available on the market.'

Maureen wasn't completely convinced. She didn't know why, but something didn't feel right.

Eva provided her with a quick demonstration on how to set up the machine and soon Maureen found herself climbing inside the Aqua massage. Oddly enough, she didn't feel at all claustrophobic. In fact, it was much more comfortable than she imagined it would be.

Laying quite still and relaxed, she waited patiently. The pump started and she immediately felt the massage jets working over her body. This is really good, she thought. The temperature rose quickly to her setting and the pressure from the water varied as they worked the different areas of her body. Maureen was like an excited school child. This is wonderful, she sighed. She closed her eyes to, as Eva had advised, "maximise the experience." The powerful jets worked strictly to her settings and the tiny fingertip massaging gave Maureen a strange orgasmic sensation, something she had never experienced before. She had read an entry in a web site forum, from a woman who claimed to have given herself an orgasm. She chuckled quietly to herself.

Suddenly the pressure went up and now the jets aggressively thumped her body. Maureen panicked, hitting the red emergency stop button, but nothing happened. She could feel the water whooshing down her back and around her feet as the human pod started to fill with water. The level rose quickly. Maureen frantically bashed at the button. The door had an automatic lock. She kicked the glass to no avail. The water rose steadily, until her head too, was immersed. Her eyes bulged as she her lungs became saturated with water. The life slowly drained from her body. She was dead.

Eva calmly walked into the room. She grinned as she opened a small tap to allow the water to drain from the pod. The door opened and Maureen's limp arm fell out, hanging lifeless over the side. The water lapped from her mouth.

She stroked Maureen's face, 'Well my dear, I did say it was an experience worth dying for.' Her hoarse laugh echoed around the room.

Black Widow

Since marrying the delicious twenty-year old blonde model, Miranda Smart, Harry Cartwright had enjoyed the most prolific sex of his life. Nine months ago, at the ripe old age of seventy-five, the multi-millionaire business tycoon took his fifth set of wedding vows. Now Miranda was about to give birth to a baby boy.

They met in the million-dollar club in Las Vegas and after a drunken night of attempted sex got married. Of course, he knew that she was only interested in his wealth and contacts. He too, was only really interested in having another pretty accessory hanging on his arm at major functions. The prenuptial agreement was more than fair.

Harry had arrived at the hospital. The white limousine dropped him at a discreet side entrance and he was immediately greeted by a very attractive private nurse – Fiona Turner.

'I'm Nurse Turner. Come this way please sir.'

'Please, let's be less formal on such a happy occasion. I insist that you simply call me Harry.'

His charming smile did nothing to stop her feeling somewhat uneasy. She knew how important he was. She was in her late thirties, still had a good, well-proportioned figure, but had to disguise the grey hairs with a little hair colouring. As they hurried down the long magnolia painted corridor, she did think it strange that he did not wish to be with his wife during the actual birth. Perhaps, he is squeamish, she thought.

'This way please sir, I mean Harry, sir,' she said awkwardly.

'Any chance of a coffee, black no sugar?'

'Yes, I will get some right away.'

He sat on the beige leather sofa in a very tastefully decorated room; the scent of fresh flowers filled the air and the soft lighting offered a calming influence. He sifted through the selection of magazines. I wonder how many of these magazines will suddenly find me more news worthy, he thought.

'Here we are, sir, I mean Harry.'

'Thank you. Now, please join me. I do not really wish to sit in this room alone.'

Fiona felt obliged and nervously poured herself a small cup of coffee. Their eyes met momentarily. They both smiled and took a sip of coffee. They both attempted to start a conversation and then laughed.

'I suspect that you are wondering how a man of my age can still manage it,' he said rather presumptuously.

'It is amazing,' she cringed, realising how rude it must have sounded.

'No not really.'

They paused for another sip of coffee. She still felt a little embarrassed, but sensed that something was troubling him. Her courage grew as natural curiosity started to take control.

'If you don't mind me asking,' she paused for a response.

'Not at all, fire away.'

'Well, how do you do it at your age? What I mean is, how you find the time, you know?' she carelessly asked. At this point she just wanted the ground to open up and swallow her.

'What you meant to ask is how I keep the old motor running?' he laughed.

'Well, yes, I guess I am a little curious,' she admitted.

'Fiona, you look the sort of person I can trust with my little secret,' he said more formerly.

'Yes, you can and I don't mean client confidentiality. Your secret will be safe with me,' she replied forcefully.

Assured by her sudden declaration, Harry lent forward,' A year or so ago, I read an interesting article in a medical journal.'

Fiona nodded.

'Scientists in Chile have found that the black widow spider, whose bite is fatal to many, but can cause prolonged and involuntary erections in men.'

Fiona listened intently.

'A research team have been studying the spider's venom for several years. According to the locals, there are tales of Chilean farmers who acquired this superhuman virility after being bitten by the black widow.'

Fiona smiled uncomfortably.

'Chilean folklore describes virile men, known to have spectacular sexual energy or many sexual partners,' he added.

Fiona nodded. Not too sure where this was going, but I can hazard a guess. What interested her more was, why a successful businessman had been reading medical journals?

'The Chilean black widow is also commonly known as the "wheat spider" as the wheat fields is its natural habitat. It is where its victims, young farmers, receive a near fatal bite. For these strong young farmers a bite leads to erections that can last for days and involve involuntary ejaculations. At the end of their nightmare, the man is left sexually energized and feeling physically stronger.'

The depth of his knowledge on the subject impressed Fiona. She couldn't help noticing some puncture marks on his arms and was desperate to ask the question that now occupied her mind.

'Furthermore,' he continued. 'This variety of black widow, which can only be found in the south of Chile, has spermicidal properties that cannot be found in black widows from any other regions of the world. The initial studies focused on using extracts from the venom to treat erectile dysfunction.'

A little thought popped into Fiona's mind that sent a cold shiver down her spine.

He went on,' So, I made a few discreet inquiries.'

'You, injected yourself with some venom?'

He laughed, 'Good Lord No. The spider's bite can kill children and the elderly. I use Viagra like everyone else.'

'Good, you were starting to scare me. I had visions of you injecting yourself with venom,' she replied, pointing to his arm.

'No – Insulin,' he answered. 'Anyway, further research discovered a molecule that also made this particular type of venom an effective contraceptive, a potentially marketable contraceptive, a therefore a great business opportunity for the creators of the spermicidal drugs.'

'Ah, I see, Viagra with the added benefit of being an effective contraceptive – clever,' she said.

'Well, I didn't become a multi-millionaire by accident or by chance. I am now funding all the future research. In fact, my entire estate has now been invested in this project – All thirty million dollars to be exact,' he revealed.

'What about your wife and the baby?'

'The baby isn't mine,' he replied coldly.

Confused, Fiona asked, 'How do you know that?'

'I had a vasectomy before the marriage to my third wife,' he replied. 'I have been sterile for a good many years now. As the saying goes, "once bitten, twice shy". The second wife was one of the other types of black widows,' he laughed.

The Level Crossing

It had been a wise move for Patricia Cunningham. The claims department was already proving to be more challenging, interesting, and far more rewarding than proposals. Today however, offered something more than just a challenge. Patricia had joined Pearson Insurance Brokers straight from school. This "no hoper", as a former teacher had once referred her to, is now carving a nice career for herself. She had transformed from her tomboyish ways into an attractive, tortoise-shell eyed brunette with a figure that now constantly drew admiring looks from the opposite sex.

She waited patiently as the somewhat dated IBM whirled into action. Her desk was located in a quiet corner of a thirty-strong office pool. Each desk was surrounded by low-level grey partitions, offering only a minimal amount of privacy. The PC rattled and squeaked, lights pulsed, and the screen suddenly burst into life.

Patricia opened a red folder marked "Case 251004". A red folder depicted that this was a multiple-claim case. She quickly glanced at the contents. The login screen appeared. The hard drive vibrated, as she entered her user ID and password. The sheer volume of the content inside the folder told her that this was not going to be quite so easy. Multiple claims always involved assigning liability, which, in the absence of a police report, was always a bit tricky. This case was particularly complicated as one of those involved in the accident suffered a heart attack and died in hospital soon after.

An unopened white envelope caught her attention. Funny, she thought. I could have sworn that I had opened all the incoming mail for this case. Patricia was very meticulous at work and it was unlike her to miss anything. It was postmarked 30th October 2007. She glanced at the calendar, that's odd. It nearly a month old and still hasn't been opened. Maybe, it got lost internally, she thought, unconvinced.

Upon opening the envelope, she found a beautifully hand-written letter. The paper was embossed with a rather official looking family crest. Patricia read the contents, admiring the very elegant style of the writing.

"Dear Sirs,

This letter is my account (as per your request) of the events that took place during the incident at Tanwick level crossing on October 25th, 2004. I would therefore be grateful if you would give careful consideration to the details herein.

It was about 9:55am and I was taking Sonny (my Jack Russell terrier) for his morning walk. As I approached the Tanwick crossing, the barrier was down and the red lights were flashing. I proceeded to the front of a short queue of vehicles to wait until the 10:00am express train had passed.

At the front of the queue there was a horse and cart. I recall that the horse appeared to be a bit jumpy. Behind the horse and cart was a red sports car, British of course! It was a warm day, so the driver had the top down. Behind the car was a motorcyclist. The rider, to me anyway, appeared to be too small for such a huge monster of a bike.

The train duly arrived on time and so passed through the small station. The sudden rush of air and noise appeared to startle the horse. It reared up and backed the cart into the front of the sports car. This resulted with some of the contents of the cart being deposited onto and into the car. The rider of the large yellow motorbike laughed so much that he/she fell off the bike and became impaled on the ground. The contents of the cart consisted of steaming manure and straw. The driver of the sports car did not find being buried in crap too amusing and dragged the owner of the cart to the grass verge. A slight fracas broke out. The horse then bolted, taking with it, the front spoiler of the sports car (including number plate: CU 4 NOW). The remaining contents of the cart were evenly distributed along the road. The fracas now turned into a brawl. The rider of motorcycle was laughing so much that he/she was unable to free himself/herself. So, at this point I felt obliged to intervene. I mistakenly and rather foolish tied Sonny's lead to what I thought was the fence. As I walked across towards the two brawling gentlemen, the automatic barrier rose, taking with it poor old sonny. Needless to say, my loyal companion, Sonny, died. I really do not know what came over me at the time, but I walked over to the motorcyclist, who by now was crying with laughter, and kicked him/her in the head. He/she then stopped laughing.

I wish that this letter be held on file to provide, to the best of my knowledge, an accurate account of the events that took place that day.

Yours faithfully

Peter Charles Morgan"

Despite Mr. Morgan's quite witty account of the incident, Patricia was not laughing. A strange feeling came over her. This job had provided her with some surprises, but none quite like this. She checked and double-checked that data of the computer database with the contents in the file. She checked the postmark, compared the signature on the letter with and that of the claimant's original policy document. 'It can't be,' she mumbled.

Peter Charles Morgan died of a heart attack that very day: October 25th 2007. She stared at the letter once more, yet this letter is dated October 30th 2007; There is no doubt about it, it is his signature, which means, that he was already dead when he wrote this letter.

Fire

'We can move in next week,' Alex said.

'Good. I am fed up living out of a suitcase.'

Since meeting Alex, life had been an unbelievable roller-coaster ride for Tania Thompson. She really loved it at Mrs Beatrice's bed and breakfast place, but she just wanted to finally set up home with Alex. They had moved nearly five hundred miles away from Northampton to leave their past troubles behind them.

'Did they say which day next week?'

'The agent said everything will be finished by Tuesday,' he replied.

Sitting in front of the rather grand mirror of the antique dressing table, Tania ran a brush through her thick black hair. Her complexion looked bleached. I really need a facial, she thought. My eyes don't look quite so blue these days, she observed. It would be nice if Alex could to take a day off to take me to Edinburgh, She sighed. Alex has already had too much time off in the past few weeks. First there was the spell in the hospital, courtesy of his jealous ex-girlfriend. She grimaced.

It had taken nearly three months to move all their furniture and for the renovation of the house. Although a restraining order had now been placed on his jealous ex-girlfriend, Tania was sure that this nightmare was not over and that she would suddenly re-appear to haunt her once more. At court, Alex's ex-girlfriend had vowed that this wouldn't be the end of it and that she was going to do whatever was necessary, to get him back. The very thought sent a cold chill down Tania's spine. Then, there was her father, who hadn't spoken to Alex since the incident last summer. It wasn't poor Alex's fault, she sighed. She realised that she was being a little selfish and that Alex too, needed to get some stability back in his life.

The clouds had broken and a weak ray of sunlight poked through the advancing gaps. Tania had decided to go over to the house to take some measurements for the curtains. Alex had reluctantly put her in charge of soft furnishings. It was a few degrees warmer and a slight southerly breeze whistled across the open green valley. Tania enjoyed listening to the birds competing for airspace and soft trickling of running water, as she gently rode her bike down the tiny country lane that followed the meandering stream. She carefully dismounted her bike at the gate. It was unusually quiet. Strange, she thought. There are no workmen at the house? She checked her watch. As she opened the gate, she thought she saw a dark figure running from the back of the house and into the trees. Odd, the upstairs windows are open. As she looked closer, she could see someone calling for help from one of the windows. Grey smoke began to waft from one of the openings. Without hesitation, she swung open the large wooden gate and ran towards the house. Her heart began to pound, as panic took charge. She slid across the newly tiled floor as she tumbled through the front door. Her breathing became heavier and laboured, as she raced up the stairs. Her thighs were burning, as she reached the top of long curling staircase. She paused momentarily and then staggered towards the front bedroom. She carefully pushed the door ajar, but when she glanced over to the window, the old woman had gone. The window closed and locked as the builder had said the day before. The protective coating still hasn't been removed. Confused, she stood motionless for several moments. It has been a trying few months. I swear, I'm losing it, she thought.

There was a groaning noise from the bedroom opposite. She turned and practically leapt through the door. Alex lay partly conscious on the floor, blood seeping from a small gash on the back of his head. I did see someone running from the house, she suddenly remembered. I didn't imagine it, she protested. Oh my god, she thought suddenly. 'Alex,' she shouted. He didn't respond. Instinctively Tania threw dirty water from a scruffy black plastic bucket over him. The cold water produced a slight response from Alex. With Tania as his crutch, Alex climbed to his feet and staggered hopelessly round in circles. Tania sensed danger. 'Gas,' she shouted, grabbing Alex's arm. They both walked unsteadily out of the room and on towards the staircase.

Alex stumbled over another bucket.

'Come on. We have to get out of here,' she shouted.' Tears began to roll down her cheeks, as she fought to get Alex back on his feet. Once at the top of the stairs, his feet were unable to connect properly with the descending steps and he tumbled once more. They both, rolled down the spiralling staircase. Tania's mouth rapidly filled with blood. Alex groaned as he crashed against a ladder. Tania somehow found some more energy, hoisted Alex to his feet, and dragged him outside. Staggering a further twenty-five metres, they both collapsed onto the gravel driveway.

There was a sudden whooshing sound, followed by a loud blast. The glass exploded from the window frames, showering glass, wood, dust and debris all over them. The fierce flames and thick black smoke quickly engulfed the house. Tania glanced back up at the window. Grey smoke billowed from the opening. The old lady she had seen earlier appeared to be waving at someone.

∼∾∽

It was then; that Tania suddenly remembered what Mrs Beatrice had told them about the original house that had once stood here, the same house they had just renovated. As she recalled, "the original house was owned by a Mrs McBride who lived alone there with her two children. One day the house caught fire and apparently Mrs McBride helped her children to safety from an upstairs window. Sadly, Mrs McBride was overcome with smoke and perished in the blaze."

In the shadow of the trees, Tania saw the silhouette of a very familiar figure. She rose angrily to her feet. Her rage grew rapidly and her blood began to boil as she stomped towards the shadowy outline.

'Father,' she shouted. 'How could you?'

Saucy Jack

It was a decision that Emma Smith had not taken lightly. She really did not want to leave the boys at home alone. It is an emergency and I have no choice, she thought. There is no one I know who can look after them for an hour or so.

Bill, her husband, had been injured in an accident at work and had to be admitted to the Royal London hospital. Although, it was not far from where they lived in Whitechapel, it did mean leaving the children at home alone. Tom (her elder son) is more than capable of looking after James, she thought, trying to reason with herself. 'James, here is my mobile phone. I will ring you the moment I arrive at the hospital.'

'OK, Mum,' James replied.

'Make sure you have done your homework, before I get back.'

'Yes, Mum,' he sighed indignantly.

Emma had issued strict instructions on the "dos" and "don'ts" to the boys, but she still felt uncomfortable about the situation.

She didn't want to take an expensive taxi. The buses were too unreliable. So, she decided that it would be easier on foot. She quickly glanced in the mirror in the hallway. The dark rings under my brown eyes, smudged mascara and the deepening wrinkles of my pale face reflect the state of my life at the moment, she thought.

She threw on an additional thick green woollen jumper, covered her red hair with a thin green headscarf. Then, she carefully put on her heavy brown woollen coat and slid into a pair of black ankle boots.

'I won't be long boys. Remember what I said, now won't you?' she asked.

'Yes mum,' the boys replied sarcastically.

I do hope they'll be alright, she pondered. Well, the sooner I get there, the sooner I will be back. She slammed the solid white front door and gave it a push to ensure it was fully closed.

Outside, the air was a little fresh. There's going to be a hard frost tonight, she thought. The cold was already making her nose run. The pollution of rush hour traffic irritated the back of her throat. Emma scuttled into Whitechapel Road. The hospital was not far. She had so many things to worry about, that she hardly any time to spare a thought for poor Bill. What has the silly sod done now? she wondered. What did the hospital mean by "serious"? Can't be that serious, else the Police would have come round, she concluded. The time passed quickly.

As she had suspected Bill's injuries, were only serious insofar as, he would have to have time off work.

Bill lay quietly in the hospital bed. His tired brown eyes still struggled to focus due the medication. His wavy grey hair provided an eerie backdrop for the abrasions on his forehead.

Four cracked ribs falling down the stairs, she scoffed. Emma wanted to stay longer, but couldn't settle, knowing that she needed to get back to the boys. She had explained to Bill that she had to leave them at home alone and that she had better get straight back.

'I'll see you tomorrow morning, then.'

Bill could only manage a feeble nod.

A couple of stray tears appeared in her eyes. She hated to leave him so soon after she had arrived, but she hadn't stopped worrying about the boys from the second she closed the front door. Tom had sounded mischievous on the phone, which now began to worry her.

A sharp chill had descended upon the streets of London. The stars shone brightly in the clear night sky. The path was starting to sparkle as the frost spread across the empty paths. The moonlight cast erratic shadowy shapes all around her, as she made her way back to the house.

As she rounded the corner into the next street, a tall dark figure suddenly appeared in front of her. Startled, her pace slowed, until she had stopped about 10 metres from him. Her heart was leaping from her chest. He stood in complete silence. Only the exhalation of his breath could be seen dissolving into the night air.

'Good evening young lady,' he said in a very smooth voice. There was not even the faintest hint of an accent.

'Evening' she stuttered.

His black boots grated on the loose stone chippings, as he approached her slowly. He was tall, wearing a long black full-length coat and a black top hat. As he stopped, she noticed that he was wearing black leather gloves. He placed his hands over the silver lion's head of a black walking cane. She tried to get a glimpse at his face, but the lapels of his coat were turned upwards, casting a shadow over his face.

'What may I ask, is such a lovely lady as you, doing walking the dangerous streets of London – alone?' He said slowly in a low voice.

'Just on my way home,' she hastily replied. She started to shiver. 'I only live five-minutes from here,' she mumbled. 'My husband is in hospital and I really must get back home to my boys' she babbled on, now almost in tears. 'So, can you pleased let me pass sir,' she asked feebly.

'The boys are fine, Emma, it is Emma?'

'Shit,' she said under breath. How the hell does he know my name? 'Yes, my name is Emma. Do I know you?'

'The name is Jack,' he paused, 'Although, others might call me Saucy Jack.'

'How do you know my name?' she hastily asked.

'Please, don't trouble yourself with detail. You need to get back to Tom and James, right?

She slowly nodded her head. Her knees began to feel weak. She wanted to run, but her legs felt like they were turning to jelly.

'Then, I think it would be wise to allow me to escort you safely home, Emma.' He raised his cane, inviting her to join him.

At this point she revisited the idea to run, but her legs were still too shaky. She could scream, but the cold night air appeared to have frozen her voice. Instead, like a zombie, she walked beside him. Her hands shook uncontrollably and all she could think of was the boys.

He walked very gracefully, each long stride in time with the cane and at a comfortable pace. As hard as she tried, she couldn't see his face or any distinguishing facial features.

He said nothing more until they had arrived at her front door, 'Here we are Emma.'

'Thank you,' she hesitantly replied.

'You probably thought I was going to kill you or something ghastly like that?'

Emma shrugged her shoulders. What can I say, he is right.

'Now, I need you to do a little favour for me.' He handed her a small white envelope. 'I want you to give this to a Detective Chief Inspector Chance, Thames Valley Police'

She reluctantly took the letter, glanced momentarily at the neatly handwritten envelope and then placed it in her pocket.

'Good night, Emma.'

'Good night,' she replied. 'Thanks'

Lemon Zest – Perry A. Simpson

He raised his cane in acknowledgement, then the mysterious gentlemen gracefully faded away into the freezing mist.

⌒∾⌒

DCI Chance looked at the handwritten envelope. The contents of the letter had disturbed him. The on-going banter over the successful arrest of Mrs Tate, in the egg timer case, was also beginning to irritate him. He had become very newsworthy, but didn't like being paraded like a proud possession by the Thames Valley Police.

He read the letter again. Chance knew only too well what it all meant. London was about to be subject to a series of horrific murders. As a child he had been obsessed with any mystery, but had always been intrigued by the speculation surrounding this particular case.

Tonight, Emma Smith was the luckiest woman in London. She had only been used as the messenger, the bearer of the challenge, the bait. The Whitechapel area will no longer be safe for women at night.

D.C.I. Chance realised that, 'Saucy Jack alias, "Jack the Ripper" has returned from the grave.

He knew that he was about to embark on his most challenging case yet and the spotlight will certainly be on him.